BOOK F

VICTORIA'S LIFE IS THREATENED BY A SUPERNATURAL TERROR FROM BEYOND THE GRAVE!

At first Victoria scoffs at the legend that Collinwood is haunted by zombies, members of the "living dead." She does not believe it possible that a shaft of moonlight striking their coffin can release two bodies buried for more than 100 years.

Yet as Victoria continues to see the strange apparitions stalking the grounds of Collinwood, and as the threats to her life become more frequent, she is forced to admit that Collinwood – and her own life – are truly cursed!

THE CURSE OF COLLINWOOD is the fifth Gothic novel in the Paperback Library's series based on ABC's DARK SHADOWS, daytime TV's most popular show.

Hermes Press

Published by Hermes Press, an imprint of
Herman and Geer Communications, Inc.

Daniel Herman, Publisher
Troy Musguire, Production Manager
Eileen Sabrina Herman, Managing Editor
Alissa Fisher, Graphic Design
Kandice Hartner, Senior Editor
Benjamin Beers, Archivist

2100 Wilmington Road
Neshannock, Pennsylvania 16105
(724) 652-0511
www.HermesPress.com; info@hermespress.com

Book design by Eileen Sabrina Herman
First printing, 2020

LCCN applied for: 10 9 8 7 6 5 4 3 2 1 0
ISBN 978-1-61345-206-6
OCR and text editing by H + G Media and Eileen Sabrina Herman
Proof reading by Eileen Sabrina Herman and Malleri Weinfeld-Geer

From Dan, Louise, Sabrina, Jacob, Ruk'us and Noodle for D'zur and Mellow

Acknowledgments: This book would not be possible without the help and encouragement of Jim Pierson and Curtis Holdings

Printed in Canada

THE CURSE OF COLLINWOOD
by Marilyn Ross

CONTENTS

CHAPTER 1

For weeks Victoria Winters had fought her desire to flee Collinwood and escape all its sorrows and fears. Now the dark old mansion by the ocean had betrayed even the happy memories it had given her, for a tragic stroke of fate had cast a dark shadow on them. It was late spring and all the Maine coastal region, including the small fishing village of Collinsport, was blooming with the promise of another summer. The lawns were showing green, the tall, old trees were in leaf and the first sweetness of the garden filled the air with fragrant beauty. Yet the beauty was lost on her.

Nor could she guess what this summer was to bring. She had yet to learn that an ominous black cloud briefly shadowing the full moon that shone down on a schooner in a West Indies harbor a century back would cross the span of years to fill her existence with an incredible terror. The beating of native drums, the practice of black magic and the voodoo curse of the zombie were still beyond her realm of experience. Yet, without knowing it, she was poised precariously over an abyss of sheer horror!

She would come to know the living dead, the undead *nvumbi* of the macabre world of voodoo. She, along with others of the Collins family, would learn not to scoff at the mystery of the zombies—the demons with staring eyes and expressionless faces who in response to pale shafts of moonlight emerged from dusty, cobwebbed coffins after a hundred years to stalk and terrorize the countryside.

There had been many changes in the grim old house known as Collinwood since she had first come there, a young orphan girl with a teaching degree, to be governess to David Collins, Roger's young son. Could she have foreseen what this remote fishing village and tourist resort held in store for her, she now felt, she would never have accepted the position.

David was a true Collins, by times moody and difficult, and then in sudden contrast a likable little boy. Victoria had somehow managed to gain his confidence, but she could never be sure of him. Roger, his blond father, had not been much help to her. Since the death of his wife, Roger had spent more time in Boston and seemed to have no genuine interest in his young son.

It was Elizabeth Collins Stoddard, his widowed sister, who appeared to care most for the boy. She had hired Victoria in the first place and it was she who dominated the forty-room old mansion, the family fish-packing business and the family itself. Her only daughter, Carolyn, not much younger than Victoria, was the only other young person in the lonely house. Victoria had come to like the girl and regard her as a younger sister.

As this spring began, both David and Carolyn were living at home in Collinwood again. Roger Collins, in one of his perverse moods, had insisted on sending David to a military academy. Victoria felt that it had been an attempt to get rid of her, but Elizabeth had insisted she remain as a companion to her. So she had stayed and now David, unhappy at the academy, was back again as her charge.

With Carolyn it had been different. Elizabeth's excitable daughter had enjoyed attending high school in nearby Ellsworth. But during the early part of the winter she suffered a minor nervous breakdown. The doctors had not been able to put their finger on its cause but felt a period of rest at home would bring her back to health. To Victoria, Carolyn did seem to be recovering, but the girl was still jumpy and found it difficult to concentrate.

Perhaps the greatest change in the immediate circle of Collinwood had been the transformation in Elizabeth. After remaining within the old mansion for nearly twenty years, she had ceased her near-hermit existence and became active in the family business and the community at large again. This had come about through Elizabeth's discovery that the husband she believed dead was alive and following the sea as a career. With her feelings of guilt and remorse removed, she had become a much more vibrant personality. Her natural matronly beauty glowed once again and she was full of plans to enlarge the family business.

It was Elizabeth who brought Victoria the news that would change her feelings about Collinwood and the course of her life. The phone rang one bleak day in March and Elizabeth had taken the call. Victoria had just finished with David's afternoon study period and was still seated at the desk in the library marking some answers to a test she'd given him when Elizabeth came into the book-lined room. One glance at the sensitive features of the dark-haired woman was enough to tell Victoria something was badly wrong.

She rose from her chair and asked, "Is there some trouble?"

Elizabeth nodded, her face pale. "Yes."

"Please tell me," she said, concerned.

The mistress of Collinwood was strangely pale as she stood there facing her. "Some dreadful news on the phone just now," she said in a strained voice. "I don't really know how to begin."

Victoria frowned. "It's all that bad?" She thought about Roger who was spending the day in Boston, and of Elizabeth's husband so long away from her. Had either of them had some kind of accident?

Elizabeth came close to her and touched her arm. "Victoria, you must be brave. I have a shocking thing to tell you. Ernest was killed in a plane crash in South America."

"No!" The bitter protest was automatic on her part; she really wasn't able to think. The idea that the young violinist she loved and who loved her was dead completely numbed her mind. Her eyes brimmed with tears and she sank despairingly into the chair. Elizabeth was saying that the accident had taken place while Ernest had been en route to Rio de Janeiro to perform. All Victoria could think about was that their dream of romance had come to this abrupt, violent end. She would never see the beloved face of Ernest again.

She had favored him over all the others of the Collins family and been closer to him. They had talked about marriage but for various reasons had postponed their plans. Now it was too late. The flood tide of her grief burst free at the realization and she gave way to great shivering, tearing sobs. Elizabeth's arms were around her as she tried to comfort her.

In the days and weeks that followed, Victoria somehow went about her duties. There was Elizabeth to help sustain her and a few good friends like Burke Devlin, the mystery millionaire of the village, who had come to mean so much to her. But it had not been easy.

Then there was the day when the small box containing a brass urn with the ashes had arrived at the old mansion. There was a simple service in the private cemetery a distance to the rear of the house and near the edge of the woods. It had been Elizabeth's decision that the urn should be buried there and a stone erected to mark the grave. Victoria couldn't have cared less. The single fact that Ernest was gone was all that mattered.

But as she had stood there between a grim-faced, bareheaded Roger and a sad Elizabeth, hearing the final words spoken over the grave, her attention had drifted for a fleeting moment to a large stone vault just beyond where Ernest was being buried. It was so much bigger and more impressive than anything else in the remote old burial ground that she momentarily wondered about it. Later she was to remember this and speculate if her sudden odd feeling had been the result of a whispered message from Ernest, a warning from the beyond that even at this moment she was moving into the shadow of an unknown horror!

In the late afternoon following the burial service she had sat in the big living room of the mansion with its portraits of Collins ancestors crowding the walls. Elizabeth sat across from her in a wing chair while Roger stood by the sideboard, a half-filled glass in hand.

Elizabeth broke the silence that had cloaked the room. "You mustn't think of leaving us, Victoria," she pleaded.

"I have this wish to get away," she'd replied disconsolately.

"It's natural that you should feel like this now," the older woman agreed sympathetically. "But later you may actually find comfort in living here."

"I can't imagine that."

"Think about it," Elizabeth urged. "You're near Ernest's old home and this was the country he knew and loved most. All his boyhood was spent in Collinsport. And much of the time he was here in this house."

"That's why it's so hard," Victoria protested. "Everything here will remind me of him."

"If Ernest were alive he would want you to take strength from his memory, not run away from it," the dark woman insisted.

"I agree with Elizabeth," Roger said abruptly. "You'll make a mistake if you run off now. In any case, you're needed with David back home again." It was typical of him that he thought of his own problems first.

"At least take some time to consider what you want to do," Elizabeth said. "I know you should do that. I'll not try to influence you. Your ultimate decision will be your own."

Victoria had responded to the kindness and wisdom of the older woman's words. "Very well. I'll stay a few weeks anyway."

"Good," Elizabeth said with satisfaction. "Carolyn needs your company too. She's still not fully herself. And I'm going to be busy negotiating for the Blair property and planning that addition to the factory."

"You can save your time, Elizabeth," Roger sneered. "Blair will never sell you his property. I've been after it for years and he's always said no."

"No harm in my trying," Elizabeth had said, glancing at her brother.

"Since you've started taking an interest in the business again you think you can manage everything your way." Roger scowled over his liquor glass. "The Blairs and our family have been feuding since the sailing ship days. He means to carry it on."

"Perhaps I can convince him it's ridiculous," his sister said calmly.

Roger gave a short harsh laugh. "You'll get nowhere with that old man. He'd rather give his land away than see us expand our plant on it. We were wrong to build so close to the Blair property in the first place."

Elizabeth sighed. "It's too late to do anything about that now, but we can attempt to reason with him."

So Victoria stayed on in the old mansion. The weeks passed; she began to feel more like herself. Most important in helping her get back to her normal self was Burke Devlin. With Ernest away for long periods she had been forced to turn to others for companionship and Burke had been her closest friend. With Ernest's death Burke now took on a new prominence in her life. She leaned on him more than ever.

It was one of those foggy nights in late May peculiar to the Maine coast. Burke had called her that afternoon and invited her to come into the village for dinner. Because she was feeling extremely unhappy again she decided to accept his invitation. The mournful droning of the foghorn pounded on her nerves and the fog itself seemed to be seeping in everywhere, bringing the damp chill of melancholy with it. Even the prospect of a table in the Collinsport hotel's dining room was preferable, although the hotel was by no means fancy. She knew she'd enjoy Burke Devlin's company and good conversation.

Carolyn was still dating Joe Haskell and when she learned that Burke Devlin was picking Victoria up, she came to her room and asked if she might ride into the village with them.

"Joe wants me to meet him at the Blue Whale," she

explained. "Then we're driving to Ellsworth for a movie."

Victoria smiled. "Does your mother approve?"

Carolyn nodded vigorously. "Yes. I told her I would ask you and she said it was all right."

"Then I'm sure Burke won't mind giving you a lift."

Carolyn's eyes sparkled. "Have you seen his new convertible? I hope he brings it tonight. Isn't it grand?"

"I've been in it a few times. It's very nice," she said, putting on a single string of pearls to set off the gray wool dress she was wearing. She knew that Carolyn was at the impressionable age where Burke Devlin's air of mystery and fast sports cars proved especially fascinating.

The other girl sighed. "I don't know why the Collins family built way out here," she complained. "Whenever you want to go anywhere you have to journey miles through the wilderness!"

Victoria turned from the mirror with a smile. "Isn't that another of your exaggerations?" she commented. "It can't be more than two miles to the main road and three miles to the village itself."

"Don't forget that you go through a section where there is nothing but woods," Carolyn said. "I say the family picked this bleak, isolated Widow's Hill for a home site just to spite those that came after them. When I marry I'm going to live in the city!"

Victoria showed amusement. "Have you discussed that with Joe? Not many fishermen live in the city."

"I'm not ready to marry yet, anyway," Carolyn said, blushing. "It's just that I'm tired of this spooky old place."

Victoria attributed Carolyn's present sullen, unhappy mood to her recent illness. Perhaps the quiet, sprawling mansion wasn't the best place for the girl to recuperate. But it was her home. She studied the younger girl with interest. "You *are* feeling better, aren't you?"

"Of course," Carolyn said hastily. "I'd go back to school right away, only there's so little left of this term that I may as well wait until the fall."

"That's true," she agreed.

Carolyn's eyes met hers anxiously. "I don't know why," she said, "but since my illness everyone seems to treat me differently. They take odd meanings out of what I say. Do they think I'm crazy or something?"

"Of course not," Victoria replied firmly.

The younger girl's eyes were still fixed on her. "I trust you, Victoria. I can tell you things I wouldn't dare say to anyone else."

"You know I'm your friend."

Carolyn took a step closer. "Since I've been back here I've

seen things!"

She stared at the girl. "What sort of things?"

"Shadows in the hallway that fade when I come close to them," Carolyn said very seriously. "The hand of a man, large and covered with hair, that reached out for me when I was strolling on the lawn the other night." She shivered. "A hand that wasn't attached to anybody!"

Victoria gasped. "You *must* be imagining those things," she told the unhappy girl. "It's just a side effect of your illness. And you're right—you shouldn't repeat such stories to others."

Carolyn regarded her with disappointment. "You think there's something wrong with my mind, too."

"No," Victoria told her. "But you're still very nervous. It doesn't take much to upset you."

"Victoria, I think Collinwood is haunted," the younger girl said solemnly.

Victoria offered her a faint smile. "All old houses are haunted by the past. You can feel it in their atmosphere, in the creaking joists that sometimes give in the middle of the night, and in the musty odor of shut-off rooms."

"I mean *really* haunted," Carolyn insisted. "I've been thinking. Do you suppose it could be Ernest's ghost that has come back now that his ashes are buried here?"

The girl's thoughtless words filled her with a pain she tried to conceal. "If Ernest's ghost were here. I'm sure it would be a friendly phantom. We would probably never be aware of his presence and he would gain his satisfaction through just being near us."

"But I have seen these things, I know I have," Carolyn worried.

Victoria stared at the troubled girl. "I hope you haven't mentioned this to David."

"Of course not. I wouldn't upset that boy!"

"Good!" Victoria gave a sigh of relief. "Now I want you to promise me you'll not dwell on such morbid thoughts. Meet Joe and go to the movies with him and have a nice relaxing evening. It will do you good."

"I hope so," Carolyn said. "And please don't tell my mother what I said just now."

"You can be sure of that," Victoria promised. "She'd only worry about you and I'm sure there's no need to." She wondered briefly if she was doing the right thing, but she knew the girl had to be dealt with carefully.

When Victoria went downstairs to wait for Burke Devlin's arrival, she came upon Roger and his young son, David, in the grand entrance way. Roger wheeled on her angrily. "Why doesn't this boy have more work to do at night?"

She glanced at David's sullen face and then his father's florid one—Roger had progressed well with his drinking for the evening. He usually started as soon as he came home from the plant. "David is so well advanced in his studies I haven't had to give him a lot of work to do in the evenings."

Roger Collins looked surprised. "Why don't you push him ahead faster? Give him extra studies."

"I think there is a limit to what should be expected of him," Victoria said coolly.

Her answer seemed to increase his anger. Then he shrugged. "It seems I've never been able to fight against the league of women opposed to me. First, his late mother spoiled this boy, then Elizabeth and now you. I should have given up and turned him over to you long ago." With that he strode back into the living room where she guessed he would replenish his glass.

She smiled at David. "Your father isn't really angry. He just wants you to be smart."

David's boyish face was pale and his expression pinched. "My father hates me," he said. "He always has."

Victoria felt a pang of pity for the child. She moved across to him quickly and with her arm around his shoulders, assured him, "You shouldn't say that. It isn't true."

The boy looked up at her. "Where are you going?"

"To the hotel for dinner. Burke Devlin is picking me up. And I'm taking Carolyn along. She's meeting Joe."

David's small face was wistful. "I wish I could go. He's got a real great car!"

Victoria winked at the boy. "I think that might be arranged for another time. I'll speak to Burke about it tonight."

"Gosh, would you?" David's face brightened.

"You can count on it."

And she kept her word. After they had left Carolyn at the Blue Whale and she and Burke had driven on to the hotel, she told him about the boy and his problems at a table in a quiet corner of the dining room.

Burke Devlin's handsome face showed his keen interest in her account of the happenings at Collinwood. He said, "I've always considered Roger rather a bully, but I hardly expected him to abuse his own son."

"I don't think he means to," she said. "But that is what it amounts to. If you could take David and me for a drive some afternoon I know he'd be thrilled and I'd be grateful."

Burke smiled. "I'd enjoy doing it. Any day I'm here you can

call me."

"You have been away more lately," she said. "I've missed you."

"That's encouraging," the millionaire said. "I'm happy to say I'll be around most of the time for the next month or two." He paused. "I don't think Carolyn is looking as well as she might."

"No. She's recovered very slowly," Victoria agreed. "Sometimes she says things that worry me."

"Such as?"

Victoria's eyes met his. "I know I can trust you not to repeat anything I tell you."

"Naturally."

She frowned. "It's going to sound ridiculous to you. But only tonight she told me she's been seeing strange shadows and other things around Collinwood. She thinks the house is haunted."

Burke raised his eyebrows. "What did you tell her?"

"I said I was sure she was imagining things. But I know I didn't convince her." She paused, forcing out the next words. "She thinks it might be Ernest's ghost."

He met her gaze silently, then asked, "Do you believe that?"

"Of course not," she said, looking down.

"Don't reply too quickly," he warned her. "I know that Ernest's death was a shocking blow to you all. This ghost business could well be an aftermath to it. I'm not suggesting that Carolyn has seen anything, but you know there is a school of thought that doesn't exclude the possibility of ghosts."

"Are you saying that you believe in the supernatural?"

He frowned in consideration. "I don't know quite how to answer you. Let me put it this way. There are things I don't understand."

She stared at him incredulously. "I've never thought of you as being superstitious."

"I'm not, in the sense you mean," he told her. "Neither am I going to shut my mind to things I can't properly explain. Spiritualists think the natural visible universe has a supernatural, spiritual counterpart that exists beyond it and is inhabited by the disembodied spirits of the dead. Nearest the earth are those earthbound because of old attachments. These are the spirits that experts claim do the haunting until they move on to a higher plane. This often takes some time."

Victoria gave a tiny shiver. "You make it all sound so logical."

"I have attended séances and seen some strange things,"

Burke told her. "I have heard mediums in a trance speak in voices other than their own and recount incidents and messages that only the dead could know. I've watched figures materialize in ectoplasm and seen infra-red photographs taken of them."

"You think that Ernest's spirit may be at Collinwood trying to break through to me?" she asked in a strained voice.

"I don't know," Burke Devlin said. "I think it would be wise for you to put all this out of your mind. That's why I've given you a hint about the vast scope of spiritualism. Once caught up in it, you may not easily escape."

Victoria stared off into the distance. "If only I could be sure," she said.

"I won't try to tell you anything more about the spirit world or ghosts," Burke Devlin said quietly. "But if you like, I'll take you to somebody who can talk to you about the phantoms that walk in the night. And who also knows more about the history of Collinwood than anyone else in the area."

She looked his way again. "Who?"

"Have you ever heard Elizabeth or any of the others talk about 'Mad Martin'?"

Victoria thought for a moment. "The nickname seems familiar." Then suddenly, "You don't mean that old, old man who has the house down by the beach not far from Collinwood?"

"That's him," Burke said. "He's at least ninety-one or two. And he can tell you some strange stories, I promise you. Would you like to meet him? His name is really Amos Martin and I've gone down to his shack since I was a boy." She nodded. "I think it would be interesting."

"Do you want to go after we finish dinner?"

"Would he be home?"

"He never leaves the place these days," Burke Devlin told her. "He's far too old and feeble."

"Would we be intruding?"

"He enjoys company. And he considers me a friend."

"Then let's go," she said.

They left the hotel as soon as they'd finished their meal. The fog had become heavier since they'd gone inside and Victoria worried about Carolyn and her boyfriend driving back from Ellsworth. The road was bound to be bad. But it could be no worse than the shore road they took to reach Amos Martin's house. Since the road fringed the ocean the fog was extremely dense there. Burke had to drive very slowly.

The strong headlights of the massive convertible cut only a short distance through the fog, dissolving into a confused blur that made the driving very hazardous. Burke gave all his attention to the wheel, his eyes straining to follow the road. She sat tensely at his side, already feeling they should not have attempted even this short drive under such adverse conditions.

"We shouldn't have come," she said.

Burke spoke without turning to her. "We'll manage," he said. "We've covered most of the distance now. The house must be only a short way ahead and on the right."

"I've seen it from Widow's Hill," she said. "But I've never been down here. What's he like?"

"Very intelligent," Burke assured her. "Of course he's mostly self-educated. His father died when he was young, but his mother lived almost as long as Amos has. Perhaps longer. I'm not sure. She was alive when I came here as a boy. They called her the witch."

"Why?"

"She was very old and thin and looked like one," Burke said, smiling in remembrance as he stared into the fog. "She held séances here in this old house. That was how Amos became interested in ghosts. His mother was known in all this part of the country as a medium. I believe she even had sessions in Boston. But by the time I knew her she was too infirm to travel."

"What a strange family!"

"They were," he agreed. "And you will find when you meet Amos that he has something unusual about him—a quality that suggests he may have been able to penetrate the veil to that other world."

Suddenly the ghostly outline of a two-story frame house loomed ahead in the fog and Burke brought the car to a halt before it. "I'm not sorry to get here," he said, turning to her for the first time since the drive had begun.

As she stared at the dilapidated old house she felt a chill of apprehension. It suggested decay and sinister secrets. "I see no light. Are you sure he's home?"

"Bound to be," Burke said. "But he has only oil lamps and they don't throw off much of a glow. I'll shut the headlights off and maybe we'll see a light through the windows." He did so, plunging them abruptly into darkness. Close at hand the surf roared monotonously.

The darkness and the sound of the waves made her shiver. "What do we do now?"

"We'll try the door," he said.

He opened the car door for her and they went over to the house. Burke knocked on the panel of the center wooden door; there was no answer. He knocked again and they continued to stand there in the damp, eerie darkness.

At last he said, "You wait here. I'll try the back."

Before she could reply or protest he had vanished in the night and she was alone. She gathered her trench coat about her and realized that she was trembling. She fervently wished that Burke had taken her with him.

And then she heard a rustle behind her. Cold terror surged through her veins. Turning slightly, she saw the blurred outline of what seemed a disembodied hand reaching out for her.

CHAPTER 2

Victoria screamed and pressed back against the door. As she did so there was a hacking, coughing sound from the fog-ridden shadows and a weird bent figure gradually took form before her eyes. The thing moved closer to her and she was about to cry out again when Burke Devlin suddenly appeared from around the comer of the old house.

Quickly he stepped between her and the creature looming in the fog. "Amos, we've been looking for you."

The racking cough came once more. And then the odd apparition spoke in a husky, low voice. "The restless ones are abroad tonight. They drove me from the house."

"It is a miserable, foggy night," Burke Devlin said. "I have brought someone who wants to talk to you."

The old man cleared his throat, but his voice was still husky. "The spirits came soon after dusk. They closed in around me and then the table was overturned. I came to the beach for refuge."

"Miss Winters wants to ask you some questions," Burke said placatingly. "Will you see us for a while?"

"If the spirits let me be." He stumbled past them through the murky night, making his way around the house.

Burke took Victoria by the arm. "He wanders at times," he warned her. "The only way is to humor him."

She leaned close to Devlin and whispered, "He frightens me!"

"Don't let him bother you. He's quite harmless and you'll find him fascinating."

Victoria very much doubted this, but with Burke's arm around her she felt less terrified. She and Burke followed Amos Martin to the rear door and inside.

Amos Martin fumbled about in the dark and finally struck a match which he touched to the wick of an oil lamp. When the wick was showing a square yellow glow he replaced the smoky glass shade with a bony hand. Now highlighted by the glow of the lamp on the sideboard, he turned to them.

He was a mere skeleton, the skin on his face so tightly drawn back that his black, toothless mouth was stretched in a perpetual grin. His eyes were small and sunken and his nose had the lines of an eagle's beak. His eyebrows and hair were scant and his bald dome rose above the patches of white hair at his temples like a Gothic arch.

His shabby clothes were filthy. He wore some kind of shapeless high boots and into these were tucked dark, shiny pants. His jacket was drab gray and any pattern it once might have had was so faded and worn as not to be discernible. He wore only an undershirt of the same dirty color underneath it. His long, gaunt face was covered with a stubble of soiled white whiskers.

He pointed a skinny finger to the overturned kitchen table. "The spirits' work!" he rasped and then he coughed again. The cough went on and on.

Burke nodded to her. "Let's repair whatever damage the spirits have done." He went over and righted the table while Victoria gingerly retrieved from the floor the things that had not been broken. When they finished, Burke drew out the several kitchen chairs and set them in the middle of the dirty, smelly room. "Now will you talk to the lady?" he asked Amos Martin.

The ancient, gaunt face turned to her and the old man sank into one of the chairs, scrutinizing her with sunken eyes. "What brings the likes of you two here on such a night?"

Burke motioned her to a chair and sat down. He leaned toward the old man so his words would be clearly heard. "Miss Winters is living up on Widow's Hill with the Collins family. She is anxious to know more about the house."

Old Amos Martin nodded. "Collinwood! It is a cursed place!"

Victoria glanced questioningly at Burke, then addressed the old man. "Why do you say that?"

"For more than a century the curse of black gold has been

upon it!" Amos Martin told her and then lapsed into another coughing fit.

When this had subsided Burke took over the questioning again. "Is Collinwood haunted?"

The old man's head weaved from side to side and the sunken blue eyes stared off into space. "It was always a place of ghosts," he rasped. "From the beginning, long before a Collins built there. It was from the Widow's Hill the womenfolk of the village came to watch the return of the fishing boats. And there was keening and moaning whenever a boat did not come back. The phantom of death stalked that cliff and stalks it still!"

Victoria was startled by the manner in which the old man's voice had risen until he was almost shouting as he finished. She said, "Please tell me more."

His chuckle sounded like a death rattle. "Aye," he said. "I will tell you more. More about Derek Collins and the curse of the black gold."

"Do that," Burke Devlin urged him. "You have spun the tale for me more than once. And it is worth hearing again." He gave her a small smile of encouragement.

"You can see the face of Derek Collins in Collinwood still," Amos Martin rasped. "He was big and dark and handsome in a rough way. And he was a devil!"

"In what way?" Victoria asked.

"When he was twenty-two he was the master of a schooner, the *Mary Dorn*. He sailed her between Portland and Barbados in the West Indies carrying regular cargo."

"His portrait still hangs in the living room at Collinwood," Burke told Victoria. "You must have seen it."

"Aye! His portrait is still there and his restless soul as well," Amos Martin agreed in his harsh rasp. "There is another portrait that should be there, but is not—his wife, Esther, whom he met in the Indies. She was the daughter of the island's governor and Derek was a dashing giant of a man who stole her heart. The story goes that he brought her back to Collinwood once, but she did not like the great black house with its chimneys stretching out to the sky like witches' claws. So he took her away and then he broke her heart."

The old man paused. His bony chin dropped on his chest and his sunken eyes closed. It was as though fatigue had suddenly overwhelmed him and caused him to collapse. Victoria glanced at Burke Devlin, who returned a reassuring nod.

"Tell us how he broke her heart, Amos," Burke said.

The gaunt face lifted and the sunken eyes opened. "It was my ma's favorite story," he said in that eerie, harsh voice. He stared wistfully toward the flickering flame encased in the smoky shade. "Ma is in this room tonight! I swear it! She and the others come around on nights such as this."

"Derek Collins, Amos," Burke prodded him gently.

"Derek was a dark-souled villain," the old man said, picking up his cue. "He was not content with the profits of regular trade. He began to ply a new route that took him from Africa to the West Indies and the South. And he filled the hold of the *Mary Dorn* with a cargo of black men! When his young wife discovered what he was doing she threatened to leave the ship and him. He deliberately tormented her by forcing her to witness the suffering and degradation of his captives until she was consumed with a hatred for him that exceeded any love she had ever known."

The old man's recital was interrupted by another session of racking coughing. Victoria waited patiently, wondering how the old man survived the dampness in his cold old house.

"They made port in Barbados on the way back to Africa," Amos Martin finally resumed. "She had a vicious quarrel with him again, begging him to give up the slave trade. He laughed at her. In despair she went to her father's house and told him her story. The Governor boarded the schooner and warned Derek Collins that he would not have his daughter involved in such a business and that unless he gave up slaving, the *Mary Dorn* could not dock there in future. Derek laughed in the Governor's face. And Esther went home with her father. The *Mary Dorn* was due to sail in the morning."

Victoria said, "And so Esther and Derek parted?"

The old man gave a cackle of harsh laughter. "Not in this world nor the next," was his surprising comment. "Esther was a daughter of the islands. She brooded about what she should do. And on that moonlight night a hundred years ago she made her way back to the *Mary Dorn* where she found her husband in his cabin. Before he could do more than rise to his feet she drew out a concealed pistol and put a bullet straight through his temple. He dropped like a felled ox!"

He paused and Burke told Victoria, "Now you've come to the most amazing part."

Martin nodded. He rubbed his bony hands together feverishly as he went on, "Esther had, already made her plans. She enlisted the help of a devoid elderly native woman who brought an island voodoo witch doctor to her. There in the captain's cabin she stood over the body of her husband and told the voodoo chief what she wanted. Derek Collins' body was to be specially prepared to live again—not as a human but as a zombie, one of the walking dead, condemned to walk the earth as mindless slaves. The voodoo man carefully went about his preparations, even sewing up the skin of the temple wound and removing the bullet so there would be no visible scars. The clouds blotted out the moonlight as the voodoo chief finished his work."

The old man paused and his gaunt face reflected the horror of the tale he was reciting. He cleared his throat and continued, "Then Esther Collins carefully explained to the voodoo expert what she would require him to do next. And when she had told him, she calmly produced the gun again and put a bullet in her own heart. As the servant who loved her wailed, the voodoo chief began his final task. Esther's body was given the same zombie preservation as her husband so that she might join him in the future when he came back as one of the living dead. It was close to dawn when the voodoo man finished with her and left the bodies side by side in the cabin."

Victoria was caught up by the story. "Who found the bodies?"

"One of the crew the next morning," Amos Martin said hoarsely. "He notified the Governor. And he came and claimed the bodies."

"Were they buried in Barbados?" Victoria asked. The old man shook his head. "No. The Governor had the bodies placed in elaborate mahogany coffins and shipped back to Collinwood for burial in the Collins family graveyard. They are still there in that big vault—the largest in the cemetery."

Victoria gave a small gasp. "I remember the vault. I noticed it the day they buried Ernest's ashes."

Burke nodded and turned to Amos Martin. "Do you really believe those bodies are still in that vault?"

The gaunt old man studied the lamp flame with his rheumy, sunken eyes. "They are there," he said. "Deep in the shadows of the vault, waiting for a shaft of moonlight to cross their coffins and stir them into life. Let even a faint touch of moonlight touch Derek Collins' coffin lid and he will burst from it as if it were matchwood. Then he'll free his wife Esther and the two will join the macabre zombie throng who stalk the earth—the mindless ones who live in the shadows to bring vengeance to the guilty . . . and death to the innocent."

Victoria sat for a long moment in silence. The story was shocking enough to frighten anyone. She had heard of zombies, but only vaguely. And she had never thought of them existing other than in Africa or the West Indies. It was utterly incredible that the threat of zombie terror could hang over Collinwood.

Burke Devlin said softly to her, "He's very tired now. I think we'd better leave him."

It was true. The old man's chin had slumped down on his chest again and he was sitting motionless as if he'd sunk into an exhausted slumber for a second time.

She stood up. "Is it right to leave him here like this? I mean, alone in this cold house."

Burke said, "I know it seems heartless. But he is used to it. It's what he expects. Any attempt to interfere with him would only upset him."

They left quietly by the rear door with the old man still asleep. Burke guided her back to the convertible and helped her in. The fog had not thinned any and when he started the engine and switched on the lights it seemed clear they would have the same difficult kind of journey back to the main road.

As he turned the car around, he asked, "What did you make of him?"

"I think he must be partly insane."

He nodded. "As you know, they call him 'Mad Martin' in the village. Yet I hardly think he's all that crazy."

"It was a strange, eerie story," Victoria said. "But I don't know whether to believe it or not."

"I've heard him tell it before," Burke said. "The details were almost the same."

"Almost?" She stared at him.

"He didn't vary in any of the important details."

"I suppose he got the story from his mother," Victoria said. "She made a living from spiritualism, you told me. Naturally she'd have a number of these horror stories to induce the right mood in those who attended her séances."

"You sound as if you're a skeptic."

"I am."

"You admit you saw the vault the day you were in the cemetery for Ernest's funeral."

"I saw a vault," she agreed. "But that doesn't mean I have to accept all of Amos Martin's fantastic story."

Burke's eyes were fixed on the blurred beam of his headlights as he headed the car back to the main road. He said, "You don't believe in ghosts, then?"

She sighed. "I suppose that's right."

"I wanted you to hear something of Collinwood's history," he said. "I felt you might be influenced by the story of Derek Collins. It seems that you aren't. You'll go on believing only what you can see and touch."

"Isn't that a good criterion?"

"Not for me," he said. "Perhaps if you visited the cemetery and saw the coffins of Derek and Esther Collins for yourself you'd be in a better frame of mind to accept that there are mysteries we do not fully understand."

"Perhaps," she said without enthusiasm.

"Will you go there with me?"

Her eyes opened wide. "Are you joking?"

"No," he said. "I've always wanted to verify Amos Martin's story. Not much use in doing so without a witness. I can't think of a more cautious witness than yourself. What do you say?"

It was put to her almost as a challenge. She smiled at him forlornly. "I didn't think you were serious at first. You really want me to go there with you?"

"Yes. The story has haunted me for a long time."

"It is macabre enough," she said with a slight shiver. "Very well, I'll go. But mostly to prove that Amos Martin's story has been elaborated."

"When?"

"Whenever you like."

"Tomorrow?"

"If it's a day fit for such a visit and you come after three thirty. I don't finish with David until then."

"Then it's settled," Burke said. "I'll meet you at Collinwood at three thirty unless it happens to be raining."

"What do you think we'll find?"

"I haven't the slightest notion."

"I think I have," she told him. "My guess is we'll discover the vault is empty—that those coffins were removed years ago."

"Perhaps," Burke admitted. With a swift glance her way, he added, "There is one thing."

"Yes?"

"I wouldn't mention it at Collinwood." His eyes were again focused on the foggy road ahead.

"Our going to the cemetery?"

"That's right," he agreed. "Elizabeth would be all right. But if it ever got to Roger you could depend on him raising objections— if only to be unpleasant. He'd have all sorts of arguments against disturbing the bones of his ancestors."

She stared at the handsome man behind the wheel. "But if they see us driving over there?"

"They needn't," he said. "I'll drive away from the house and take a side road back to the narrow one leading to the cemetery. We can walk part way."

"You make it sound so conspiratorial," she said.

"It's a touchy business," he reminded her. "And the Collins family can be difficult when it comes to something like this."

She knew it to be true, and she agreed that Roger might go

out of his way to stop them from investigating the vault. Especially in the mood he'd been in recently. Although it made her feel she was playing some trick on the family, she realized it was probably the best way. There was nothing harmful in what they planned to do.

They had reached the end of the shore road and now Burke turned the car out into the main highway which they'd follow until they came to the private road leading to Collinwood. There was little traffic on the four-lane road and the few cars there were crept slowly through the fog.

It took more than twenty minutes to reach the mansion on Widow's Hill, dark except for the light which had been left on over the outside door. Burke got out of the car to help her to the top of the steps. She fumbled in her purse for her key.

He smiled at her. "Don't forget tomorrow."

"I won't."

Burke took her briefly in his arms for a goodnight kiss and then she let herself inside. Having his friendship, she reflected, was perhaps the most important thing in her life these sad days since she'd lost Ernest. In Burke Devlin she'd found a patience and understanding that were rare.

Yet even he had a certain mystery about him. There were many rumors as to the source of his sudden wealth. Of the many wild conjectures, Victoria preferred to believe the most widely accepted one—that he'd had fantastic success as a stock speculator. He certainly had plenty of money and was doing a lot for Collinsport with his various enterprises. All in all, he didn't seem to be the kind of person usually interested in spiritualism.

It gave her a weird feeling to think that the two tragic figures of that long-ago night in the West Indies might actually be resting not far from the old mansion. Of course she didn't believe Amos Martin's story that the voodoo-treated bodies were there in the dark shadows of the vault awaiting only moonlight to release them. But she was interested in finding out if the coffins had actually been shipped to the remote private cemetery. Finding them would at least confirm part of the strange old man's eerie narrative.

Next day the sun had come out again and it was much warmer. Elizabeth drove off to the factory in Collinsport shortly after one o'clock. As Roger was away on a business trip to Portland, only Victoria, Carolyn and David were at the house, along with the dour manservant. Carolyn was up in her room reading when Victoria finished working with David in the study.

As she closed the lesson book she smiled at him and said,

"Mr. Devlin promised me he'd take you for a drive in his new convertible soon."

"When?" David demanded eagerly.

"I can't say exactly," she told him. "Any time after today. I'm seeing him today, but we have some other things to attend to."

"He's coming here this afternoon?" The sullen expression had returned to his small face.

"Yes. But he has some work to attend to. So we'll have to wait until another time for your drive."

David grabbed his study books and hurried to the door. "I don't care if I ever ride in his old car!" He rushed out, slamming the door.

Her pretty face took on a look of displeasure. She didn't want to upset the boy and yet often it was almost impossible to avoid it. David was so touchy! He had a good deal of his father's uncertain disposition.

To avoid keeping Burke Devlin waiting, she quickly changed her clothes and went out to stroll in the garden until he arrived. He didn't keep her long. His convertible appeared on the private road leading to the mansion almost on the dot of three thirty. Her excitement rose as she stood watching his car come along the cliff and considered the nature of the adventure ahead of them.

There was no one in sight at Collinwood as she got in the car, so Burke decided to take the narrow road around the mansion and outbuildings that led to the private burial ground on the edge of the woods.

"Nobody at home at all?" he asked as he drove.

"Only Carolyn and David and they're inside somewhere." Burke gave her a smiling glance. "I half expected not to see you."

"Why?"

"I thought you might change your mind. I know cemeteries aren't exactly your favorite place to spend an afternoon."

"I said I'd come," she reminded him.

"So you did," he agreed as he brought the car to a halt at the bottom of the field. "We'll have to walk the rest of the way."

Even on this bright afternoon the sight of the cemetery with its rusty iron fencing and tilted gravestones cast a spell over Victoria. Walking at Burke's side she became silent, her thoughts brooding and far away. She thought of Ernest, whose ashes were buried in this lonely place and whom such a short time ago she'd expected to marry. She began to regret that she had agreed to this forlorn visit. A quartet of crows rose quickly from the tall dark forest on which the cemetery bordered to circle gracefully above the evergreens, uttering their melancholy cries.

The entrance was barred by a chain suspended between two

battered gray concrete posts. As Burke lifted the chain for them to pass through he said, "You're suddenly so quiet."

Victoria forced a smile. "I'm sorry. You were right about cemeteries depressing me. Especially this one."

"I understand," he said quietly. And he took her arm to guide her toward the large granite vault without taking her directly past Ernest's recent grave. Grateful for this consideration, she kept her eyes fastened on the vault.

"Do you think it will be locked?" she asked.

"I'm not sure," he said. "I hope not. I'd hesitate to tamper with a lock without at least discussing it with Elizabeth."

"I agree," she said quickly and began to hope the century-old vault would have a stout padlock and they could leave the melancholy place at once. It made her flesh creep.

The vault stood seven or eight feet above the ground and had a rusty iron door at one end, about five feet high. All around the imposing granite monument were lesser stones and markers dating back to the middle of the nineteenth century.

Burke's handsome face showed his excitement as he left her to go ahead and examine the rusty door. After a moment he turned to her triumphantly. "There's no padlock!" His voice seemed to have taken on a hollow, odd note since they'd entered the cemetery. There was a strange, unnatural quality about their surroundings and the sun had vanished suddenly behind clouds. A coldness came over her, as if she'd already entered the tomb.

He pointed to the latch on the rusted door. "That should offer no problem," he said. He gave her a teasing glance. "Are you ready to open Pandora's box?"

"I don't know," she said quite seriously. "I've never considered that a very amusing story."

"Too late to turn back now," he said. "We'll soon know whether Derek and Esther Collins are here."

She gave him a frightened look. "Burke! Should we disturb them?"

He laughed. "You sound as if you really believed Amos Martin's story now—and you were the skeptical one!"

"I still am," she said. "But I don't like interfering with this vault. It seems close to desecration."

"I promise you I'll show the greatest respect," he said. "That is, if we manage to open this door. It may not be as easy as it seems."

He tried to force the latch up. Flakes of rust fell from it, but it didn't move. He exerted more strength, the result was that his hand slipped and he gave his knuckles a bad skinning. With a murmur of annoyance he tried again. This time the latch raised with a grating sound.

"At least that's done," he said with satisfaction, and swung the rusty door inward. It creaked mournfully as it gave way, revealing the dark opening of the vault. Even from where Victoria was standing she could smell the dampness and stale air of the burial crypt.

Burke took a small flashlight from his pocket and gave her a questioning look. "Well?"

"Do you want me to go with you?" she asked in a faint voice.

"That's the whole point of it," he said. "I want a witness." And he waited for her to join him. "Watch, there are two or three steps down."

They entered the dank tomb together and stepped down into the darkness. Burke directed the flashlight beam to scan the small enclosure. And on granite shelves at either side of the tomb there rested large oaken coffins.

Victoria gasped. "They *are* here!"

"So it would seem," he agreed and stepped close to the coffin on the right. He brought the beam of the flashlight to the brass plate on its top and scraped away the dust and cobwebs so he could read the engraved lettering. "Derek Collins, 1859."

Victoria stared at the shadowy outlines in awe. "So that is his." Her voice echoed strangely in the vault.

Burke nodded. "That is where the giant Derek rests," he agreed, his voice having the same ghostly hollowness as her own. He went across to the coffin on the opposite shelf and again cleared away the accumulated dust and read aloud, "Esther Collins, 1859."

"Then the story must have been true."

He shot her an enigmatic look. "Every bit of it, I'd say—including the part about their being given the zombie treatment. That's why the mahogany coffins have been enclosed in these stout oak casings and the covers nailed down so securely."

He had barely finished speaking when there was a sudden rustling sound from the coffin in which Derek Collins rested. Victoria gave a cry of alarm and pressed close to Burke.

CHAPTER 3

Burke's arm was around her. "You *are* jumpy!" he said, scanning the area from which the sound had come with his flashlight.

She was trembling. "It sounded as if he was moving in his coffin!"

"Nothing like that," he assured her. "More likely some kind of rodent we've alarmed. It's scurried into a dark corner until we leave."

Her heart pounded less furiously. "Let's get out of this dreadful place," she said in a tense voice.

"In a minute," he said. "I'd like to examine these coffins more closely." He left her to do so. Then he returned to her with a perplexed expression on his face. "I wonder..."

"Wonder what?"

"If those other coffins are in the outer boxes. I thought at first that the lids were nailed down, but brass screws were used." He glanced at her. "I think we'll have to make another visit here. I'll bring a screwdriver and other tools."

"Don't count on me."

"You don't want to leave a job half finished," he said. "I want to see if the actual caskets are inside those cases. You know, there have been rumors that when Esther's father sent the bodies back he used the coffins to hide a large amount of gold coinage he'd come upon in Derek Collins' cabin—money he wouldn't touch, as it was loot from the traffic in slaves. That money was never found. And according to one version of Amos Martin's story, the gold is still in these coffins."

Victoria frowned. "You know it's just another legend. Let's leave here and shut the vault and try to forget about it."

He turned the beam of flashlight on Derek Collins' coffin again. "I'd like to do that. But my curiosity won't let me. I'll come back alone or with you and discover what those oak cases are covering."

Finally he turned rather reluctantly and escorted her up the three stone steps to the outside again. She welcomed the fresh air and drew it deeply into her parched lungs. The sun had not shown itself yet, but even the cloudy day was preferable to what she'd just emerged from.

Burke Devlin was busy with the rusty iron door, which resisted his efforts to close it. Finally he got it two-thirds of the way and then it stuck. He stared at it and offered her a despairing look. "No use! I've tried everything. That door won't close without some work. I'll have to leave it that way until I come back."

Victoria studied him with alarm. "Please don't talk about coming back."

"I mean to. I have to now. I can't leave the door that way. The place would fill with debris."

"You should never have gone into that vault," she said seriously, her eyes meeting his.

"Why?"

"I'm sure it will bring us bad luck," she said with a tiny shudder. "Both of us. And what I heard moving in there didn't have to be a rodent."

His eyebrows raised. "You're a lot more superstitious than I suspected."

"The evil that Derek Collins created in life surrounds him in death. I'm certain of it," she went on bitterly. "Let's get away from here as quickly as we can."

"Of course, if you feel that strongly about it," he said, all consideration once more.

They walked swiftly from the cemetery and she said nothing until they left the cluster of grassy mounds and headstones behind them and were crossing the field to the car.

Then she said, "I'm beginning to believe there is something in what Amos Martin told us. I had the weirdest sensation when we were in that vault—as if I was being watched by eyes filled with hatred!"

"Dead men's eyes?" he scoffed gently.

"All right!" she told him defiantly. "Dead men's eyes, if you like. Amos Martin claimed they had been given treatment to make them living dead. I'm sure those zombies were staring at us from their caskets."

"And this is the girl who only believes what she can see and touch," Burke said with amazement, opening the car door for her to get in.

They took the side lane back to the main road leading to the mansion, although it was a roundabout route. It hid the fact that they were coming from the direction of the cemetery, and Burke was upset about the partly open door and more anxious than ever that the Collins family shouldn't guess what they'd been doing.

"We'll have to get back there tomorrow," he said as he drove. "I don't want to leave the door ajar."

"You don't need me to go with you when you fix it," she said.

"I do," he insisted. "I want to take another last look inside before I close that outer door."

She stared at him in dismay. "You just won't be satisfied until something truly dreadful happens!"

He glanced from the wheel. "Such as?"

"I don't know. Death, maybe! Or a dread disease. You remember the curse that followed those who defiled that Egyptian king's tomb."

Burke chuckled. "You're not putting Derek and Esther on a par with the pharaohs, are you?"

"I think there is as much evil around that vault as you'll find anywhere," she said. "I'm sure there is a curse upon those two and anyone who interferes with them."

He brought the car to a stop at the front entrance of Collinwood. "Until we meet at three-thirty tomorrow," he said, smiling.

"I've not decided yet," she said, her hand on the door. "I may never go back there again."

"You won't be able to resist it."

"Don't count on that," she warned him as she got out.

He leaned across to her. "Be sure to say nothing in the house. We don't want them down on us before we have a chance to finish our investigation."

She shook her head. "I've never seen you so interested in anything before. It's not like you. Are you thinking about the gold you might find in those coffins?"

"I have all the money I'll ever need."

"Then why?"

"It has become a kind of challenge to me," he admitted. "I'll never rest until I know the full truth about what is in there."

"There are some truths better left hidden," she reminded him.

He smiled. "Back to Pandora again," he said. "Isn't that where we began?" He waved, turned the car and drove away.

When Victoria mounted the front steps the door suddenly swung open for her. The surprise on her pretty face gave way to a smile when she saw it was Elizabeth holding the door. The older woman had returned home before her.

"I was watching you two from the side window," Elizabeth said with a twinkle in her eyes. "I'm glad you've found some male company again."

Victoria felt suddenly shy. "He's very nice."

"I call that an understatement," Elizabeth said dryly. "I can tell you've made a conquest. I could read it in his eyes. Burke's in love with you."

"Oh, no!" Victoria protested. "We've always been friends."

"That may be what you think," the dark woman said with a faint smile. "But I bet if I should question Burke he'd admit he was in love with you."

"Please don't!" Victoria begged.

"Don't worry," Elizabeth said. "I won't embarrass you." She glanced toward the stairway. "When I came home I couldn't find anyone. Carolyn and David must both be upstairs."

"I think so," she agreed. "Carolyn was up there reading when I left a short time ago. And David has probably gone up to work at his studies."

"Come in and sit here awhile," Elizabeth invited her. "And tell me how David is coming along with his studies. Roger complains you don't assign enough work for the boy to do."

Victoria followed her into the large, luxurious living room. "It's not fair to say that," she protested. "I give him all the work he needs."

"I had an idea you did," Elizabeth said, seating herself on one end of the Italian Provincial sofa and indicating that Victoria should sit there with her. "Roger enjoys causing trouble. You've been here long enough to know that." She sat down and studied Elizabeth with admiring eyes. The smart beige dress with its black accessories set off the older woman's dark beauty. She said, "I like your dress."

"It's one of my own favorites." Elizabeth smiled wearily. "But it didn't do me any good today. I called on old man Blair about buying his property and I have never before been treated so rudely. Simon Blair practically ordered me out of his place. He had the nerve to say that all the Collins family had been rogues since Derek Collins' time."

Victoria almost gasped at this unexpected mention of the man whose tomb she had just come from. Regaining her poise, she managed, "Wasn't that an odd thing for him to say?"

The older woman sighed. "It's a long story. To make it short, the story goes that Derek Collins was in the slave trade. He and his young wife died strange deaths in the West Indies. That's his portrait, almost directly across from you."

She looked quickly in the direction Elizabeth had indicated and saw the portrait on the paneled wall. Dark in tone and framed in gold, it showed the bold features of a large young man whose mocking eyes seemed to leer at her from under heavy black brows.

"I hadn't noticed him before," she said, her gaze still fixed on that cruel face.

"We don't point him out to guests," Elizabeth was quick to admit. "The family has always felt he disgraced the name. He *does* look rather coarse, doesn't he? But I hardly expected Simon Blair to hark back to slave days as a means of insulting me."

Victoria forced herself to turn from the powerful portrait and say, "It wasn't very considerate of him."

"He's not a considerate man," Elizabeth mourned. "This feud between our families has gone on for generations. But I'd hoped we were all sensible enough now to forget about it. I must admit Roger warned me."

Victoria smiled ruefully. "No doubt he has had his own problems with Blair."

"He has," Elizabeth agreed. "Well, I must find another way. I'm determined to enlarge the plant. And the Blair land is vital to my plan. I'm going to try talking to his lawyers. Maybe they can reason with him."

"That might be a good idea," Victoria agreed, her eyes returning to Derek Collins' mocking glance.

"You seem fascinated by that painting."

"I think I must have heard about him before," Victoria faltered, making herself look at the older woman.

"Quite likely. He's buried here in our own cemetery. You must see his vault one day. It's very elaborate. His wife is buried with him. Poor thing! She was a West Indian. I don't believe she could have had much happiness in her marriage. My father told me that when the bodies were brought here there were all kinds of weird rumors in the village. They claimed the two had been changed into zombies and would roam the countryside, killing and destroying. But we've never been bothered by their ghosts."

Of course not, Victoria answered silently, *you've never been subjected to any unpleasantness because those two have remained at rest in their vault. But let them be awakened and you'll have a taste of the terror that zombies can impart.* She said, "People tend to exaggerate terribly."

"Especially in those days," Elizabeth agreed. "I don't know what was done with their bodies before they were sent up here from Barbados, but I'd be willing to bet it was a kind of embalming to preserve them for the long voyage and nothing more."

"Quite likely," Victoria said politely, although convinced that the "embalming" had been done by a witch doctor.

After a few minutes they both went upstairs to prepare for dinner. Victoria found herself haunted by her strange experience in the vault and the portrait of Derek Collins. The moment she had heard that rustling from the giant young man's coffin was chillingly vivid in her memory.

She fervently wished she had been able to dissuade Burke from taking her to the vault—and she knew she would go again tomorrow. He would have to go back to fix the door and would probably resent it if she didn't go with him. She had never seen him so obsessed with anything before; it was unhealthy. As unhealthy as her own fixation concerning the portrait in the living room. Had Derek Collins truly some strange power that reached out from the grave and possessed people?

All during dinner she said little. Afterwards, Carolyn tackled her about it in the hallway. "Are you ill, Victoria? You look pale and you hardly said a word at dinner."

Victoria attempted a smile. "Spring fever, I guess. I didn't realize I was all that quiet."

"You were," Carolyn insisted, staring at her with questioning eyes.

"What are your plans for the evening?" Victoria asked, anxious to change the subject. In her light blue mini-dress with matching stockings and hairband, Carolyn looked much too elegant not to be expecting company.

"Joe plans to come over for an hour or so. We'll talk and stroll around outside. It's warm and there'll be a moon tonight."

"Romantic!" she teased the younger girl.

"It will be," Carolyn said. "What are you going to do?"

She shrugged. "Nothing. I'll read for a little and go to bed."

Carolyn's eyes twinkled. "You do your courting in the afternoons. I saw you drive off with Burke Devlin."

Victoria blushed. "We only went for a short drive."

"I think Burke is really special. I'd grab him myself if I were old enough," Carolyn continued innocently.

Victoria made some laughing comment to this and went on into the library. She stood for a moment staring at the shelves and then without selecting a book she went to the stand with the dictionary and opened the volume close to the back cover. Running her finger along the z entries, she searched until she came to *zombie*.

She read quickly: "zombi, zombie, a corpse brought back to life by supernatural agency. Haitian Creole, zobi. African, Congo, nsumbi, devil." She closed the book and turned away. Had the movement she'd heard from the coffin been a warning that Derek Collins was truly one of the living dead, restless to break the confines of his mahogany casket and the outer oaken box in which some wary Collins ancestor had sealed him?

Until she'd listened to the weird old man in his beach hovel she'd never known anything about zombies. Now her thoughts were filled with strange fears and premonitions.

When she'd studied that portrait of Derek Collins earlier she almost felt it had come alive, that Derek's grimly mocking smile was a warning of what might be ahead.

Pushing aside these thoughts, she selected a mystery novel with a London setting and started upstairs to her own room to enjoy an hour or two reading before she went to bed. Lately she'd had all too few opportunities to sit down with a good book.

Dusk was turning rapidly to darkness as she adjusted the lamp by the easy chair in her room and sat down to read. She soon lost all sense of time; her absorbed reading was only broken when a mournful howling intruded on her.

It was such an eerie, unusual sound that she put down the book, waiting to hear if it would come again. Probably it was some stray dog baying at the moon.

Baying at the moon! When Carolyn had earlier predicted there would be a moon tonight, she hadn't taken any notice. Now she was terrified. She got up quickly from the chair and hurried across to the windows. When she drew the drapes apart, there in all its glory was the full moon reflecting down on the ocean! She stood staring at it, remembering the eerie howl of some minutes before.

And she was remembering much more than that. What was it old Amos Martin had said? The two zombies were resting in their coffins waiting for a shaft of moonlight to free them. Waiting for the release that would come when the moonlight streaked across their coffins and they were freed to wreak their vengeance on the countryside. And all she could think of was that

Burke had not been able to close the rusted door of the vault.

That door was partly ajar and the bright moonlight could surely seep into the shadowed tomb! Had that been the meaning of the inhuman howl that had roused her from her reading? Had she heard the cry of a zombie, one of the living dead emerging from the tomb? Was Derek Collins free after a century in his casket? And would Esther be able to roam at his side and terrorize them all?

Her eyes were on the perfect moon again and she tried to convince herself that she was allowing her thoughts to run wild. This was a night for lovers, not for the living dead. She had let a superstitious old man fill her mind with nonsense. She must not give way to this weakness.

With firm resolve she pulled the drapes closed again and went back to her chair and book. But she could no longer keep her mind on her reading. Nervous and upset, she wondered just who was in the old house with her besides the boy, David. He would be in bed and asleep by this time. Carolyn would still be out with Joe, probably. And both Elizabeth and Roger were off somewhere.

Matt Morgan would be in his room, but she wouldn't turn to that surly character for help. Her chances of reaching Burke Devlin on the phone would be slim. And yet she felt desperately in need of someone to talk to. Again she put down the book and rose from her chair.

A few minutes later she was in the downstairs hall and then out on the steps. The moonlight was so bright it had almost the clarity of day. And far off down along the beach she could see the sagging outline of old Amos Martin's house. A daring thought crossed her mind. If she took the path down the cliff to the beach road she could walk to Martin's house in fifteen minutes. He would be glad to talk to her and tell her more about the unknown. She'd almost made up her mind to go see him when she remembered there would be the walk back alone. It would be foolhardy to expose herself to such danger.

Abandoning the idea, she continued to stand on the steps and stare out across the lawn and the ocean beyond the cliffs. The distant pounding of the waves had long since become familiar to her and she did not mind their melancholy. The light of a buoy showed on the water.

And then she turned to gaze in the direction of the road. For a fleeting second she saw two shadows that struck horror in her. Two shadows moving side by side, one much larger than the other. And then the shadows were gone and she was staring with fear-widened eyes at a group of medium-size evergreens. There could have been nothing there, she tried to tell herself. But she knew different. For just that one moment she had seen figures moving toward the road.

She quickly went inside and closed the door after her and leaned against it weakly. How could she allow her fears to take such control over her? She was being foolish! Imagining things that weren't there! Seeing ghosts in every shadowed place! She would have been disdainful of it in anyone else and here she was allowing herself to go to pieces.

A sound from the stairway made her start and look up with frightened eyes. To her utter relief it was David in his brilliant scarlet pajamas. She moved toward the foot of the stairs and asked, "What are you doing up, David?"

"I woke up and there was a bright moon," the boy said. "So I went to the window and I thought I saw you and Burke out walking."

She frowned. "You're wrong. I haven't been further than the steps. You likely saw Carolyn and Joe."

"No! I know Carolyn and Joe, they're both about the same size," the boy said scornfully. "This was a big man like Burke with a small lady at his side. They were heading out to the road."

The familiar cold chill surged through her again. But she mustn't infect the child with her own terror. In a voice that trembled only slightly she said, "Well, whoever you saw, it's time you were back in bed. If your father comes and finds you on the stairs he'll punish you and discharge me. So get along!"

"All right!" David said sulkily and turned and went back up to his room.

She watched him go with a sigh of relief—a relief that passed almost at once. The two shadows in the moonlight. . . And then a strange thing happened. As if a magnet was drawing her she found herself walking toward the wide doorway of the living room. The big room was in darkness, but as she entered it she became aware of the moonlight coming in through a window whose drapes had not been drawn. And the shaft of fight cut a path across the room and hit the opposite wall to cast a weird highlight on the portrait of Derek Collins!

She froze as she stood there staring at it. It was like a message, but a message she didn't want to receive. More than anything else she wanted to turn and run from the room, but she was paralyzed with terror.

The spell was broken by the front door being flung open and she wheeled around to see a white-faced, frightened-looking Carolyn standing in the hallway. She hurried out to greet the girl.

Carolyn had closed the door and now stood staring at her

in surprise. "I can't believe it!" she exclaimed weakly.

"What is it?" she asked, afraid to hear anything more but knowing she must ask.

"I had an awful fright out there!"

"Go on!"

Carolyn swallowed hard. "I said goodnight to Joe and waited until he drove out along the road. Then I started to walk back across the lawn. Something, someone came at me from the shadows."

Victoria stared at her. "Are you sure?"

"I'm positive," Carolyn said. "A giant of a man! He came straight toward me, with his hands outstretched!"

"Did you see his face?"

"I didn't wait to get a good look at him. I raced toward the door and hoped it would be unlocked. Luckily it was!" Carolyn looked as if she might be ill.

"It had better be locked now," Victoria murmured and proceeded to do it. Then she turned to Carolyn again. "Are you sure you really saw this giant?"

"I did! Please believe me!" The girl cried.

Victoria glanced toward the stairs. "We mustn't disturb David," she said. "He's already been on the stairs once. And we don't want to frighten him needlessly."

Carolyn's eyes were wide. "Not needlessly! There's some giant madman on the grounds!"

"You think," she said wearily. "You told me the other day you had seen strange shadows and a hairy, disembodied hand. You must realize some of these are fancies. Your nerves have been jumpy since your illness."

"It's not my illness," Carolyn said. "I know what I saw."

Victoria swallowed hard. She believed the girl was right but didn't want to let her think so. It would be the worst possible thing to allow the nervous younger girl to know that she and David had also seen figures on the lawn. So she said, "Try to forget about it for tonight. You're safe and maybe by tomorrow there will be some explanation for it."

"Aren't you going to call the police?"

"I'll see. I should wait until your mother gets back from the village," she said.

"Mother out in that station wagon alone!" Carolyn wailed. "That giant might wave her down and murder her!"

"There's no point in allowing yourself to panic!" Victoria remonstrated. "Your mother is capable of looking after herself."

Whatever response Carolyn might have made to this remained unspoken—both girls were frozen into silent horror by a sudden pounding on the front door.

The loud pounding continued. Both girls looked at each other, then at the door. Then a familiar voice began to roar and curse. It was Roger!

Victoria opened the door and the blond man stood there glaring at her. "What's the matter? You deaf?" he asked drunkenly.

"I wasn't sure who it was," Victoria apologized.

Roger Collins came in with an unsteady step, his face flushed and his eyes not completely in focus as he continued to scowl at her and Carolyn. "You two here talking and letting me cool my heels out on the steps. A man doesn't dare leave his keys behind in this house or he's liable never to get in!"

"You could have rung the bell," Carolyn admonished him, "instead of doing all that terrible pounding!"

He smiled at her sarcastically. "Smart girl! Exactly like your dear mother!" he snapped. "When I want in here I let people know! And I let them know any way it pleases me! It pleased me to pound on the door!" He turned and made his way unsteadily up the stairs.

When he was out of sight, Carolyn shook her head. "I guess that's about all that can happen for one night!"

Victoria nodded. "Maybe he was your giant."

The younger girl furrowed her brow. "No." But there was a note of uncertainty in her voice.

"You look awful," Victoria told her. "Please go up to bed. I'll wait for your mother."

Carolyn hesitated. "You feel sure she'll be all right?" Victoria was again forced to offer an assurance she didn't feel. "Of course she'll be all right."

"Very well," Carolyn said with a slight yawn. "I am dead on my feet." And she started for the stairway. She turned and added, "If she doesn't get home soon let me know."

Victoria promised she would. Carolyn said goodnight and went on up to her room. Left alone, Victoria felt her nervousness gradually return. She paced up and down in the hallway and worried about the unexplained things she had seen and heard about. And she began to think that some harm might have come to Elizabeth.

When she was almost ready to phone the village, she heard the sound of the station wagon's tires on the gravel of the driveway. Elizabeth had driven right up to the door, which wasn't her usual custom. The bell rang; Victoria opened the door.

Elizabeth's lovely face was distorted with fear. "I had a terrible experience," she said in a shaky voice. "A man and a woman tried to stop the car. When I slowed down I saw their faces. They were horrible. The man was a giant with hair down around his ears and the woman had a mad smile!"

Victoria listened numbly as her eyes moved from Elizabeth's pale face to the full moon showing over her shoulder. What terror had been unleashed tonight?

CHAPTER 4

Elizabeth came inside and Victoria closed the door. "Will you leave the car out front for the night?"

"Yes," Elizabeth said. "I wouldn't dream of taking it to the rear parking lot with those creatures prowling around. Bolt the door."

Victoria did so, torn by the guilty feeling that she should tell Elizabeth about the cemetery vault and what she feared the consequences of exploring it had been. But she was certain that the older woman would dismiss the zombie story as nonsense. So she decided to say nothing until she had talked it over with Burke Devlin the following afternoon.

She asked Elizabeth, "Where did you first see them?"

The dark woman fingered the front of her light topcoat nervously. "Just as I left the road for the grounds. They suddenly sprang out of the bushes in front of the car—this giant, hairy man and the tiny woman at his side."

"What did they look like?"

A gleam of incredulous horror came into Elizabeth's eyes. "It's hard to explain," she said. "They were like beings from another world. Or at least they seemed so in the moonlight."

Victoria ventured another question. "How were they dressed?"

Elizabeth gave her an odd look. "It's strange you should mention that," she said. "Their clothes were unusual. The man had on some sort of uniform like you see these hippies wearing. You know, all gold buttons, braid and epaulets, and the woman had on something white and flowing. I've seen folk singers dressed that way with hair like hers, long and loose about the shoulders. But she had this peculiar vacant look in her eyes and a set smile."

"Perhaps they belong to the hippie group that found their way here from Boston," Victoria suggested.

"The girl might have been high, I suppose." But Elizabeth's description of the clothes sounded to Victoria alarmingly like what a nineteenth-century sea captain and his wife might have worn. Had Derek and Esther Collins finally escaped from the grave?

"I don't know who or what they were," Elizabeth said, still white and upset. "I can only tell you they had an aura of evil about them. As soon as I saw him towering up ahead of the car with that long black hair and mocking smile on his coarse face I knew he wasn't to be trusted. I pushed my foot down on the gas pedal and spurted the car ahead and past them."

"They fell back when you kept on driving?"

Elizabeth nodded. "Yes. I saw the big man wave a fist at me and heard him shout something. Then they stumbled back. A moment later I was here in the driveway." She moved over to the window next to the door and pushing aside the curtain, peered out. "They still must be out there somewhere now."

"You weren't the only one who noticed them," Victoria informed her. "Carolyn thought she saw a giant man emerging from the bushes as she watched Joe drive away."

"There you are!" the older woman said triumphantly. "I know we have prowlers or tramps of some kind around. I'll call the police in the morning."

"Perhaps they'll be gone by then," Victoria suggested, not sure she liked the idea of Elizabeth appealing to the police. If they began investigating and saw the vault had been tampered with they might begin asking some troublesome questions.

"I'm exhausted," the older woman complained as she started for the stairway. "You have no idea what a lot that scare took out of me."

"I can imagine," Victoria said dryly, remembering her own moment of terror.

Elizabeth turned to her from the stairs. "Make sure everything is locked. We don't want to risk their breaking in here."

"I'll take care," Victoria promised.

Elizabeth continued to stand there a moment longer with a thoughtful expression on her face. "I don't know what it was. There was something different about those two." And she turned and continued on up the stairs.

Victoria watched her vanish in the shadows of the first landing and again she was tempted to call out to her, to tell her she thought she knew the identity of the two intruders—perhaps to ask her if she had noticed any resemblance between the giant in the shabby uniform and the mocking face of Derek Collins' portrait. But once more she crushed the impulse to speak and instead busied herself with the task of making sure all the doors were locked.

When this was done she turned out everything but the night light and started up the broad stairway. In the shadowy light of the single weak bulb the old mansion became really sinister. And pausing halfway up the stairs with her hand on the banister, Victoria stared with frightened eyes at her own tall shadow on the wall. Collinwood was a house of ghosts. Amos Martin—Mad Martin—had termed it a cursed place. And perhaps it was. She continued on up to her room.

Her sleep was restless and disturbed by phantom figures. Once she awoke to the darkness of her room sure that someone was standing by the bed staring down at her. But she could see no one and so dismissed it as part of a nightmare. But she did not sleep well and felt weary the next morning as a consequence.

Elizabeth joined her in the kitchen as she was preparing breakfast. The dark woman's face was bright with excitement as if she'd just learned some secret. She told Victoria, "I listened to the Portland news broadcast as I dressed and I feel sure I know now who those two were who tried to wave me down."

She was taken back. "Who?"

"A lumberjack known as Big Tim Mooney escaped from the jail in Ellsworth last night. His girlfriend Nora Sonier was waiting in a stolen car to help his getaway. They found the car in the ditch only about three miles from Collinsport. It broke down and they abandoned it. The police have been searching around Collinsport all night."

Victoria listened with growing interest. "I suppose it could be them," she said dubiously, although she was by no means convinced.

Elizabeth gave her a surprised stare. "Of course it is!" she exclaimed. "The description fits exactly. They said he was wearing makeshift clothes and she had long blond hair. And he is a giant, just like the man who shook his fist at me!"

"You say he was in jail at Ellsworth?"

"Yes. Waiting trial for murder."

"Murder!" Victoria echoed. "Then he'd really be dangerous!"

"Worse than that," the older woman said, "the story on the radio described him as somewhat retarded and dangerous when drinking. And it stressed he has abnormal strength! How lucky I didn't stop. I'll have to phone the Ellsworth jail at once."

"Yes, I suppose, so." Returning to her duties at the toaster, her mind reeling with the new development, Victoria could say nothing more.

All the talk at breakfast centered on the escaped criminal and his female companion. Even Roger joined in the discussion. Victoria said little, since she still felt this new happening had set Elizabeth off on a wrong track. But she meant to discuss her convictions with Burke Devlin and see how he felt about them.

Shortly before eleven the Ellsworth police sergeant arrived in a black sedan with the police crest on its doors and a red, rotating light on its roof. He was a heavy-built, middle-aged man with double chins and shrewd blue eyes in a bronzed face. Elizabeth told him her story first and then Carolyn and Victoria added what they thought they had seen. The interviews were held in the living room and David was kept out of it on Victoria's suggestion to Elizabeth.

"What he'll have to contribute won't add to our evidence," she argued. "And he's at a bad age to be upset about such things." Elizabeth had agreed with her. So when the police sergeant came, Victoria sent David to the study to work on his lessons, much to his disappointment.

"I never get in on any excitement!" he complained as he flung himself in the chair behind the desk.

Victoria smiled at him from the doorway. "I'll tell you all about it later. And it's the kind of thing you should be glad to miss."

So now she and Elizabeth sat on the long divan while Sergeant Sturdy paced back and forth on the heavy carpet in front of them. His weathered face wore a scowl and his hands were clasped behind his back.

At last he halted and faced them to say, "What you've told me suggests Big Tim and Nora were here last night," he admitted. "But we also have witnesses who claim they were miles away on the other side of Collinsport."

Elizabeth showed the strain of the interview. "But couldn't they have been both places at different times? From what you say, the reports didn't place them that far apart."

He shrugged. "I don't know. You may be right. It's possible they found some transportation we don't know about. Maybe someone gave them a lift and drove on and we haven't heard about it. Mooney worked in this area and knows every foot of it. Our guess is that he's hiding out somewhere here."

"On our place?" Elizabeth asked worriedly.

"Not necessarily," the sergeant said. "But somewhere in the area. Now he'll have to forage for clothes and food. So he'll be making himself known to someone. We think that's our best chance of getting him."

"Is he dangerous?" Victoria wanted to know.

"Right now I'd say yes," the sergeant said. "He's on the run from a serious charge. He may even have liquor with him. And when he's sober and cornered he's a bad fellow to tackle. He has abnormal strength and knows how to use it. You'll be wise not to venture out alone until he is apprehended."

"What about the girl?" Elizabeth asked.

"She's as vicious as they come."

"Then none of us are in a pleasant position," Elizabeth said. "When they get desperate enough they'll raid the nearest house."

"Likely," Sergeant Sturdy agreed.

"But couldn't they have decided not to remain here?" Victoria suggested. "They might consider it too dangerous and have gotten a lift somewhere else. They could be miles away from here by now, in some other state."

"They could," the police officer conceded. "But I doubt it. We've had the roads blocked. I don't see how they could have gotten a ride without our knowing it."

"But there is a chance," Victoria persisted.

Sergeant Sturdy gave her one of his quick, shrewd glances, the blue eyes fairly boring into her. "You seem very positive they've gotten away," he said. "Is it just a hunch or do you have some proof?"

She blushed. "No proof, Sergeant. I simply don't think they would stay in this part of the country with such an intense search going on for them here."

He stared at her glumly. "You may be right," he said. "But on the other hand, he knows this area well. And he knows the people and maybe some of their habits. In other words, he can use his knowledge for his own benefit and maybe last longer hiding here than he could anywhere else."

"I see what you mean," Elizabeth said. "And you're probably right. What can you offer us by way of protection?"

Sergeant Sturdy looked embarrassed. "We have our men pretty well spread out, ma'am," he said. "But I'll arrange to have a patrol car come out here every couple of hours after dark sets in."

"Every two hours!" Elizabeth gasped. "That's hardly enough."

"I agree, ma'am," he said unhappily. "Still, it's the best I can manage while this crisis is on."

"We only need protection while the crisis lasts," Elizabeth acidly reminded him.

"You can always phone the office and we'll get someone out here right away," Sergeant Sturdy assured her.

Carolyn, who had been in for part of the questioning and gone out, now had returned again and was standing in the doorway with a sardonic smile on her pretty face. "Not much satisfaction in that, Sergeant, if I've already been strangled by your murdering giant."

The sergeant turned toward her with an unhappy expression on his tanned face. "We'll just hope that won't happen, Miss Stoddard."

Elizabeth rose and gave the police officer an icy stare. "It seems most of our protection is based on hope, Sergeant."

"I promise to do my best," he mumbled. "Let me know if anything else happens."

"I trust we'll be able to," Elizabeth said in the same angry manner. "When one reads newspaper accounts of mass killings, it isn't hard to imagine what might happen here if two desperate criminals attacked us."

Sergeant Sturdy twisted his cap in his hands. "I agree, Mrs. Stoddard. I'm sorry."

Elizabeth saw him to the door while Carolyn came into the living room to join Victoria. Carolyn said, "Not much satisfaction there."

"I didn't think there would be," Victoria said. "Mother's in a rage and I don't blame her."

Victoria was on her feet. "Perhaps they've gone," she suggested. "They may never come near here again."

Carolyn stared at her. "Know something?"

"What?"

"All the time the sergeant was talking about that killer Tim Mooney and his girlfriend I had the impression you weren't interested at all."

Victoria raised her eyebrows. "What gave you that idea?"

"By your face, for one thing. You looked bored and as if your thoughts were miles away."

"Perhaps they were."

"Why should they be, if you were as worried about this Mooney as the rest of us?" Carolyn went on. "And then you talked of him and his girlfriend having moved on, as you did to me just now." She paused and asked dramatically, "What I'd like to know is, if you don't believe it was Mooney and that girl wandering around the grounds last night, who do you think it was?"

Victoria was unable to answer. She swallowed hard as she

tried to think of some suitable way to put Carolyn off. At last she said, "I haven't made up my mind."

"But you do suspect someone else?"

"I didn't say that."

Carolyn smiled wisely. "I can see you're not going to tell me yet. But I'm sure you know something I don't know."

Elizabeth returned to the room after seeing the sergeant off and gave them both a questioning look. "What is this that Victoria knows?"

"Nothing, Mother," Carolyn said quickly. "We were just talking about where Tim Mooney and that girl might be by now."

"Oh!" Elizabeth didn't look as if she fully believed the explanation, but showed no sign of making an issue of it as she said, "I think the best thing for all of us now is to try and forget about this dreadful business. It's clear the police aren't going to help us."

Victoria went back to the study and proceeded to give David a full account of what the sergeant had said. He listened with a solemn face until she had finished.

Then he said, "I think the police are crazy."

She smiled. "Whatever makes you say a thing like that?"

"It wasn't Tim Mooney and his girl here last night," the boy said with disgust. "I saw from my window. It was ghosts!"

"David!" she scolded him. "People don't believe in ghosts!"

"I do," he said stubbornly. "And I know they were ghosts, because watching them made me feel all creepy."

She decided the best way to handle it was to make fun of him. "Very well," she said. "You tell the sergeant it was a ghost when he comes back."

David showed disgust. "He's too stupid to believe it!" Which, in a way, was Victoria's own thought, she realized to her astonishment. But she made no comment as they continued with his schoolwork. As the day went on and the time for meeting Burke Devlin drew near again, she became quite nervous. She was relieved when she was able to send David off to play. She changed into a gray pants-suit and went out to meet Burke along the road so he wouldn't have to drive up to the house. It was even more important that they avoid that today.

She wondered how much Burke had heard about the previous night's happenings and if like her he would connect it with their visit to the vault. She had not thought she'd ever want to see the tomb again, but now she could hardly wait to inspect it and learn if there was any basis for her fear. By the time Burke's car came in sight she had walked far enough so their meeting could not be seen from Collinwood.

He registered surprise on his handsome face as she got into the car beside him. "I didn't expect to meet you way out here," he said.

"I was afraid Elizabeth might comment on your coming today," she told him. "Use the side lane and keep away from the house. In fact I'll walk back from the lane after we visit the cemetery."

Burke glanced at her. "Why all the mystery?"

She gave him an urgent look. "Surely you've heard what's been going on."

"You mean about the escaped murderer and his girlfriend? What has that to do with our visiting the cemetery?"

"It could have a lot to do with it. We had mysterious figures here on the grounds last night. I saw a strange shadow and Elizabeth was threatened by a man and a woman who she believes were Tim Mooney and Nora Sonier. She's even had the police here."

Burke gave a concerned whistle. "I didn't hear about that. I know the police are looking for the two in the Collinsport area and have a dragnet out for them, but I didn't guess they showed themselves here."

"I'm not sure that they did," Victoria replied grimly as he drove the car cautiously along the bumpy surface of the lane.

He frowned at the wheel. "Then who was here?"

"I thought you might be able to guess," she said in a dry voice.

Burke brought the car to a halt in the field as he had on the day before and gave her a startled look. "Would you mind explaining yourself?"

"There was a full moon last night and you left the door of the tomb partly open."

"So?"

"Amos Martin said that Derek Collins and his wife Esther were zombies waiting for a shaft of moonlight to release them from their coffins."

The young man beside her gasped. "You can't believe that!"

"The descriptions of the people Elizabeth saw exactly fit Derek Collins and Esther."

"You must be joking!"

"I only wish I were."

"You were the one who was so skeptical," he reminded her again. "I just don't get your sudden conversion."

"Things have happened that I can't ignore," she said, reaching for the door handle. "Let's get over to the vault. I'm anxious to see it."

Burke stared at her. "You really don't expect to find

anything wrong there?"

"I want to see it," she said firmly and got out of the car. Burke had brought a tin toolbox along. He got this from the trunk and silently joined her in the short walk to the cemetery. Stooping under the chain of the gateway as they had the previous day, they made their way between the grim array of graves and headstones to the vault. The day was dark, and the clouded sky held a suggestion of rain.

Burke glanced around. "Everything seems serene enough," he said, with almost a hint of relief.

She looked at him. "Always remember that coming here was your idea."

"You're the anxious one today."

They came to the rusty iron door at the end of the vault and she saw that it was still partly ajar as they had left it. Or was it a trifle more open? Her heart began to pound. Burke took the flashlight from his pocket and went ahead. He once again had to exert his full weight against the heavy door to make it move. It gave away with a complaining groan and he stepped down into the vault itself. She followed after him.

Burke stood there frozen with surprise, his mouth slightly open as the beam of his flashlight fell on the coffins. The oak covers were in splinters and one of the coffins had fallen on its side on the floor. Even the inner mahogany caskets had been savagely broken open. The tomb was a shambles.

Victoria was the first to speak in a low voice. "Well?"

Burke didn't reply for a moment. Then he said in a dazed tone, "Who would do this kind of vandalism?"

"I think I know," she said quietly, her fear lost in the satisfaction of having her theory confirmed. "Derek Collins."

He gave her a startled look. "You're suggesting that a man a hundred years dead did this?"

"I'm saying that when the moonlight came into this tomb last night he broke open his own coffin and then Esther's," she said in a dull voice. "Now two of the living dead are terrorizing Collinwood and the area."

"Madness!" Burke argued. He stepped forward to examine first the casket that still rested on its ledge and then the one that had fallen to the floor of the tomb. He knelt by it so he could read the brass plate on one of the splintered sections of wood.

"This is Derek's coffin," he announced as he stood up again.

"Of course," she said. "That is why it's on the floor. His struggles to free himself would have to be the most violent."

He eyed her incredulously. "You talk as if all this was true."

"It has to be," she said, meeting his gaze directly as they

stood there in the shadowed gloom and stench of the vault. "Who else could have done this? What other logical explanation can there be?"

"Vandals," he said.

"What would they be doing here?"

"Someone must have seen us here yesterday," he said. "They must have thought we had come to take away some valuables."

She shook her head. "There was no one around here yesterday."

"No one that we saw," he reminded her. "Yet don't forget that Tim Mooney and that girl were on the run and hiding out in this district somewhere."

"You're asking me to believe they were hidden somewhere here when we arrived yesterday?"

"Yes."

"That's almost as difficult to accept as my zombie theory seems to be for you," she said bitterly.

"Not quite," he objected. "Mooney knows the countryside well. This would be an ideal place for him to hide during the day, away from the village and the main road."

"Granting that," she said, "how do you explain the damage to the coffins and the missing bodies?"

He frowned, running his flashlight over the shattered coffins again. "I think that is simple enough," he said at last. "Mooney worked in Collinsport long enough to hear the various legends. He would certainly have heard about the gold buried here along with Derek and Esther Collins. Mooney probably decided to rip the coffins open and see if the story was true. He could certainly use the gold."

"Where would he find tools for the job?" she asked.

Burke stepped forward again and his flashlight searched among the wreckage. He bent down quickly and brought up a huge rock with a sharp edge. "My guess is that he used this caveman weapon," he said. "He had no qualms about damaging the cases as I had. If I'd wanted to be as ruthless I could have achieved the same results with a similar kind of emergency tool."

Victoria was amazed at the way he met each of her arguments, but she was not ready to give up her theory. "What about the missing bodies? You haven't explained them."

"There were no bodies," Burke said calmly. "I've believed that all along. That is why I came today to open the outer cases and the coffins. I don't think the bodies ever left the West Indies. The same voodoo witch doctors that worked on Derek and Esther Collins stole the bodies before they left Barbados."

"Why?"

He sighed. "My guess is that Esther was loved by the native servants who worked for her father. They wanted the body of the young girl to remain on the island. They took Derek's body as well since he'd been given the zombie treatment."

"And the gold?"

"They probably took that, too. Those natives knew the value of gold. All that came up here were weighted coffins. I suspected it from the beginning. It's what I wanted to prove."

"You haven't proven it to my satisfaction," Victoria told him.

"Everything I've explained is logical," he insisted.

"*If* you include Tim Mooney and his girlfriend in the picture and we don't know that they should be. And *if* I take for granted your idea that the natives stole the bodies."

"You'd rather think that under the influence of the moonlight last night those two escaped from their coffins to roam the countryside as zombies."

"The living dead," she said. "Corpses reanimated to live again as mad destructive things."

Burke had gone forward to the coffins again. He was closely examining the one on the shelf. "If I'm right about the bodies being stolen I should find something in this coffin," he told her as he searched. Then he gave a small cry of triumph as he held up a repulsive black object in his hand—a shiny thing that seemed to vibrate as he shoved it toward her. "It's a mummified frog," he said. "I knew they were bound to leave something of the sort in place of the body. It has a meaning in their ritual."

"Put it down!" she begged and drew away from him to back up the steps into the welcome fresh air. She waited while Burke rummaged in the vault for minutes longer.

Finally he came outside to join her. A grim smile on his face. "I told you," he said. "I found another one in Derek's coffin."

She stood there silently staring at him. The wind sighed through the nearby forest of tall evergreens as the first drop of rain hit her cheek. Very quietly, she said, "I won't argue with you. But there is one thing I want. I want to talk to Amos Martin. And now!"

Burke Devlin offered her a faint smile of astonishment.

"All right, if it will make you feel any better. But first let me try to finish up here."

Using a chisel he had brought with him, he spent several minutes working at the rusted door and getting it back in its proper place. This time he succeeded; when they left, the latch was closed again.

Occupied with troubled thoughts, they said little as they drove along the lane to the road and then further to the beach road. At last Amos Martin's weather-beaten house came into view.

When they left the car and went around to the rear door they found it open. And the frail old man was resting on the untidy sofa in his kitchen. He raised himself up as they entered and with a smile on his emaciated face he said, "I know why you are here. I saw Derek and Esther Collins last night."

CHAPTER 5

Victoria had hardly expected such a prompt confirmation of her theory. She stood still for a moment in amazement and then turned to Burke Devlin. Burke's handsome face was registering mixed shock and annoyance.

He moved across the small room to stand by the old man's cot. "You can't really believe you saw two people dead over a hundred years," he said.

The thin, eagle-like face showed amusement. "I met Derek Collins walking along the beach last night," he said in his harsh rasp. "And his wife Esther was at his side."

Burke frowned. "There were two criminals loose around here last night. It must have been them you saw."

"Let Amos tell his story," Victoria said sharply.

The old man nodded to her. "I know it was Derek. I recognized his face. And he wore his captain's coat—the one he had when he sailed that last voyage."

"How would you know about the coat?" Burke demanded.

"I've read accounts of it all," Amos Martin said, not to be shaken from his story. The rheumy, deep-set eyes stared off into space as he went on, "The moon was full. I was on the beach and I saw their shadows first. Him, broad and big and her, tiny at his side. They came straight across the sands toward me and I halted and watched as they passed."

"Did they give you any sign?" Victoria asked.

"They didn't have to," Amos Martin said. "I stood and watched and they went right by me without even looking at me. Their eyes had a kind of glaze and they were staring ahead of them like zombies do."

"It was Tim Mooney and his girl," Burke insisted.

The old man didn't appear to be listening to them. He gazed off into space and seemed to have fallen in a sort of trance. "They went off into the shadows," he said in his weird voice. "And there was the stench of the grave about them."

Victoria wanted to return the conversation to a more practical level. She asked, "What time did you see them, Amos?"

The rheumy eyes glanced up at her. "Long after dark."

"Around ten or eleven o'clock?"

"It could be," the old man said. "I have no watch."

Victoria turned to Burke. "That's about the time they were seen at Collinwood. It fits."

"And doesn't prove anything," the young man told her. "According to the police, they were spotted on the other side of Collinsport around nine o'clock. If a passing truck or car picked them up, it could easily have been Mooney and that Nora who showed up here last night."

"I don't think Mooney or his girl were ever on this beach," Victoria said firmly. "And I don't believe Amos does either."

Burke sighed. "Is that why you wanted to come here? To have him confirm what you've already made up your mind is true?"

"No. I hoped he might feel well enough to hold a séance for us."

The young man frowned. "A séance?"

"Why not? Maybe then we can learn something about what went on in that vault. Perhaps he could even contact Derek or Esther."

"Because I happened to say there were things about spiritualism that interested me and which I couldn't explain, you're using it against me," Burke said bitterly.

"That isn't true," she said. "What about the séance?"

He looked at her with resignation. "All right," he said. "I'll ask him." He gave his attention to the old man on the cot, who had fallen into a dejected silence. "Amos, could you hold a séance for us now? Miss Winters is interested in finding out more about the zombies."

Martin's face was grim. "She'll find out enough before it is over. Their souls have been stolen from them and they can never rest."

Burke asked again, "What about a séance?"

Amos nodded his bald head. "We can call on Ma. She's my contact. And she will tell us."

The dingy room had become darker with the advent of the storm. Now the rain that had begun in the cemetery was coming down hard and the steady downpour could be plainly heard in the untidy kitchen. Victoria was filled with an ominous foreboding. Now that Amos Martin had agreed to the séance, she wasn't sure whether she wanted to go on with it or not.

Since the old man had not risen from his bed, Burke asked, "Are there any special preparations which must be made, Amos? Let me help."

The old man stirred. Grasping the back of a nearby kitchen chair with a bony hand, he laboriously lifted himself to his feet. He went into a hacking coughing spell again; when he had finished, he stood there weakly for a moment before speaking. "The windows must be covered, the room darkened and the table cleared. We will all sit around it." Burke at once began clearing the kitchen table of the accumulation of dishes, partly eaten food and old newspapers. Victoria went to the window and placed opened newspapers across it to hold out the light in a very temporary way. When Burke had cleared the table to its greasy oilcloth covering, he set a single lighted candle in a battered holder in the middle of it.

Amos Martin's bald head nodded in approval. "That will do nicely," he said. "Now if you will sit with me at the table."

Burke Devlin gave her a strange look and once again she feared that they might be taking another step into an unknown horror. They had made their initial error in invading the ancient tomb in which the bodies of Derek and his unhappy bride had rested for so long. Would the séance be a mistake of the same kind? Or would it, as she hoped, cast a fresh light on the eerie events of last night?

Burke seemed very much on edge. "Please sit down," he ordered her.

She did so and then old Amos Martin sank into the chair next to her. He bowed his head and rested the palms of his hands on the table. He seemed engaged in some kind of bizarre prayer. Burke quietly sat in the chair opposite her, his face showing annoyance in the flickering light of the candle.

The only sound that broke the silence of the room for a moment was the continuing rain. Then Amos Martin raised his head and fixed his sunken, rheumy eyes on her.

"Place your hands on the table, miss," he told her. "Flat, with the palms down." He turned to Burke. "And you as well, young man."

They both obeyed. Victoria asked, "What happens next?"

"If we are fortunate, I shall be able to reach my mother," the old man rasped. "Then I will ask her questions. And I will refer your questions to her."

There was silence again. Victoria listened to the patter of rain and waited. Suddenly the old man began a wailing exhortation. She could not understand all his mumblings but a word caught now and then told her he was addressing his dead mother. Once more she felt a chill of fear spread through her. When she glanced across at Burke's grim young face, she felt guilty that she had insisted on going through with her scheme.

The old man's sharp cry startled her. His head slumped to one side, his eyes were closed, and the black gaping mouth had slacked open more than ever. She was sure something dreadful had happened to him. She looked imploringly at Burke, who touched a warning finger to his lips for her to be silent. So she forced herself to sit there waiting in the near darkness.

A dampness seemed to have seeped into the room and taken hold on everything. She felt its macabre hand on her and she knew that she was trembling. In a moment her teeth would be chattering from sheer terror and she would jump up and scream.

A strange gurgling sound from the old man riveted her attention and increased her apprehensions that he had been taken with some kind of seizure. And then, without opening his eyes or moving, he began to speak in a weird, high- pitched voice with a singsong quality quite unlike his own. At first Victoria could make out nothing he said. Then suddenly the jumble of words cleared and she heard him say quite clearly, "It is wet and I am cold out here! Cold and lonely!"

She looked at Burke in terror—again he motioned for her to be quiet. So she turned to the death mask of the eagle-faced old man and waited for more words to tumble from those dried, dark lips.

They came again in the singsong tone. "Amos, it is your Ma! I want to go on. I do not want to be bound to the earth any longer! I do not like to wander like this in the rain!"

The last words were loud with anguish. And then Burke surprised her by suddenly speaking up in his resonant young voice, "Mrs. Martin, we are seated beside your son. Can you hear me?"

"Yes," the singsong tone of Amos' long-dead mother replied.

"Miss Winters and I are anxious to discover something," Burke went on. "Have Derek and Esther Collins risen from their graves?"

Victoria waited tensely for the answer that might come. Then the strange voice issuing from the gaping black mouth said, "Derek Collins was an evil man! I fear him even here! I cannot say what I would! He is evil! Beware!"

The final word of warning came as a tormented scream that made Victoria gasp, breaking the spell. Almost at once old Amos raised his head and stared about in odd bewilderment.

"Was I asleep?" he asked in his familiar rasping voice.

"You were in a trance," Burke told him.

The ninety-year-old touched a bony hand to his temple. "Yes, now I remember," he said. "You asked me to try and reach my Ma. Did I do it?"

Burke nodded. "Yes. We talked with your mother for a moment."

"I thought I had gotten through to her," the old man said, glancing about the shadowed room. "I can still feel her close to me."

Burke stood up. "I think we'd better be going now. It's getting late."

She rose at once, still shaken from the weird experience they'd just gone through. "Yes, of course," she said quietly.

Old Amos Martin stared up at her. "Did Ma tell you what you wanted to know?"

Victoria swallowed hard. "Yes," she said. "I think so."

A harsh chuckle shook the veteran's bony frame. "Ma never fails."

"Thank you," Burke said with an abruptness Victoria had not noticed in him before. As he spoke he tossed several bills on the table before the old man.

Victoria remembered the windows. "I'll take down the newspapers." She hurried over to do it. Even the gray light that came in through the dirty panes of glass on this grim, rainy day was better than the chilling darkness.

Burke was waiting at the door for her. She hesitated and called across to the old man, "Thank you, Amos." But he had retreated into a world of his own. He remained seated there with his back to her, still staring at the flickering candle. Burke motioned for her to join him and she did. They scurried arm in arm across the yard in the drenching rain to reach the dry comfort of the car.

When they were safely seated in it and Burke had started the engine, he asked her, "Well, are you satisfied?"

"I'm still terrified," she said. "That was my first séance."

The young millionaire smiled grimly. "You wanted it and I

try to please."

As he headed the convertible up the shore road she gave him a faintly triumphant look. "Amos Martin's mother did mention Derek Collins. She said he was an evil man and she was frightened of him even in that other world. And she warned us about him."

"That she did," Burke said, an amused look on his handsome face as he kept busy at the wheel. "Amos put on quite a performance and I paid him well."

"Performance?"

"That's what it was. I had no idea he'd learned the technique so excellently from his mother. Or that he still had the wits and energy to put on such a show. That's why I left him a good fee."

She stared at him incredulously. "You're telling me that was all faked? It wasn't a true séance?"

"As true as most séances. Still a fake."

"I don't believe you," she said hotly. "You were telling me a different story a few days ago."

"A few days ago you didn't have this hang-up on spiritualism." He gave her a warning glance. "I watched you while Amos was going through his routine and you were eating up every word of it."

"You asked the questions," she reminded him. "You behaved as if you believed in him, too!"

"I had to play my part, after you'd gotten me into it," he said.

She turned from him to stare out at the gray, angry ocean and the whitecaps as the waves dashed in on the rocky shore. "I haven't changed my mind. And I'm not sure Amos was faking."

Burke wheeled the car onto the main highway. "I'm still betting on Mooney."

So there was a stalemate between her and the man she liked so much and whom she had come to depend on. Neither of them was willing to switch sides. Victoria blamed him for involving her in the vault business in the first place, and she felt guilty in not being able to tell Elizabeth what had gone on. But she hesitated to do so now with everything so confused. Later, she intended to make a clean breast of it.

But for the moment she supposed it would be best to remain silent. It was bad enough for Carolyn and young David to fret about a mad murderer being on the loose, without their dreading the horror of the living dead.

At the door Burke suggested, "I'll come back later and we'll drive into the village. An hour at the Blue Whale might cheer you up."

Thinking about the crowded, noisy cocktail lounge, Victoria hesitated. "I'm not sure I'm in the mood."

"It's precisely because you're not in the mood that you should go," he told her. "Having some people around you will do you good. I'll come by about eight."

"No later," she told him. "I want to be back here early." She went inside. She saw no one as she hurried upstairs to get ready for dinner. The dark, rainy afternoon suited her own somber mood. She was confused and resentful toward Burke, who had first encouraged her to a belief in spiritualism and was now suddenly taking an opposite stand. Yet she supposed he was doing it for her own good. He knew how melancholy and introspective she'd been since Ernest's death and perhaps thought her attitude unhealthy.

At dinner the talk still centered on the escaped murderer and the girl who had helped him in his getaway. Roger Collins seemed especially titillated by the jail break and the police dragnet that had followed it.

"They'll not catch them," he predicted from his place at the end of the table. "This Tim Mooney is too smart for the police."

Elizabeth frowned at him. "I don't see how you can side with a criminal who might have killed me last night if I'd been foolish enough to stop the car."

"I'm not siding with him," Roger said, his face shading with annoyance. "I'm stating a fact. The police haven't caught up with him yet."

"Surely they will," Carolyn spoke up. "They know what he looks like."

From his chair next to Victoria and across from Carolyn, David spoke with the enthusiasm of the very young, "They say Mooney is a giant."

"He is," Carolyn assured the boy. "I think he must be seven feet tall. When he came after me last night I couldn't believe it!"

"Mooney is six feet five inches, to be exact," Roger told the girl. "At least, if you can believe what you read in the newspapers. I know your mother doesn't." He glared down the length of the table at Elizabeth.

His attractive sister sighed. "Things are bad enough without deliberately trying to make them worse. I'll not feel safe in this house until those two are caught."

"They say the girl is a looker," Roger went on taunting his sister. "She's one of the hippie crowd with long, yellow hair and a great figure."

Carolyn nodded. "I read that in the paper. And Mooney wears his hair long too. Like those poets in the coffee houses."

"Like the LSD crowd that goes around killing innocent people," Elizabeth reproved her daughter. "Mooney is a kind of degenerate revered by the foolish youngsters in the Village and then in Cambridge, when he moved to the Boston area. They called him the lumberjack troubadour because he worked in a lumber camp for a few months and plays a guitar. Don't forget he killed someone and probably won't hesitate to kill again."

"It said on the radio tonight they broke into a farmhouse on Crane Road and got a lot of food and things," David said excitedly.

"Crane Road!" his mother exclaimed. "That's only about five miles from here. When did that happen?"

"This afternoon some time," the boy said. "They don't know for sure. But when the people who owned the farm came back from a trip to Ellsworth they found they'd been robbed."

Elizabeth addressed herself to Carolyn. "I don't want you seeing Joe until this scare is over."

"Oh, Mother!" The girl rolled her eyes in exasperation.

"I mean it," Elizabeth insisted. "I won't sit here worrying about you while you're out somewhere with that boy. You two would just be bait for those awful people. They'd probably kill you and steal Joe's car."

David's eyes were sparkling as he asked his mother, "Gee! Do you really think they'd do that?"

Elizabeth sighed. "Let's not talk about it anymore. I've already lost my appetite."

Roger gave Victoria a teasing smile. "It seems to me there's one person who's hardly had a word to say. What's the matter, Victoria? You too frightened by Tim Mooney and his girlfriend to offer an opinion?"

"I haven't any to offer," she said in a subdued tone.

"You're being wise," Elizabeth commended her.

Victoria smiled faintly but said nothing, the truth being that it was discretion that had made her remain silent. She had never been worried about Mooney or the girl. She was sure they must be hiding out in another part of the district, perhaps closer to where they'd made their afternoon raid on the farm—if they *had* been the ones to make the raid. She was too caught up in her fears that she and Burke had unleashed the horror of the zombies on Collinwood to think of much else.

Two hours later when she and Burke were seated across from each other in a booth in the rear of the busy Blue Whale she told him how she felt. "I think we're to blame for what's happened," she said. "And, even worse, for what may happen."

He smiled at her over his drink. "So you're sold on the

zombies."

"Yes."

"The whole nonsense will end when Mooney and that girl are captured," he promised. "You'll see."

The jukebox with its neon rainbow of lights struck up a new tune and the dancers in the back of the lounge began their wild gyrations again. The place was crowded on this wet night. The patrons were mostly young people with here and there a scattering of older fishermen, who stood mostly at the crowded bar. In a way Burke had been right. The noisy cluster of people and the warm, smoke-filled air of the lounge made it hard for her to concentrate on the cold vault from which the bodies were missing or the thought that two of the living dead might even now be converging on Collinsport.

She said, "You brought me here to change my mood."

"I considered it worth trying."

"Don't you feel any guilt for what we did?" she asked. "I'm ashamed to face Elizabeth knowing what I do."

"Of course I don't feel guilt," he said. "Because we did exactly nothing. You've conjured this business of zombies escaping from the vault out of Amos Martin's wild stories. I tell you, the people don't call him 'Mad Martin' for nothing. I made a mistake ever taking you there."

His reassurances were beginning to convince her that she might indeed be imagining it all. She smiled, "I wish you hadn't taken me to meet him."

"At least have sense enough to see it all realistically," he begged.

"What about all that damage in the vault? The missing bodies?"

"Mooney."

She couldn't make it all fit that neatly, but she said nothing. She sipped her drink and watched the dancers. As her gaze wandered to the packed bar and the entrance, she saw Sergeant Sturdy come in. The thickset officer nodded to the bartender and very slowly made his way along the length of the lounge. When he came by their booth a look of recognition crossed his tanned face as he saw her and he stopped.

"Good evening, Miss Winters," he said, adding with a wry smile, "I hope all is well at Collinwood?"

"It was when I left," she said, returning his smile with a faint one of her own. "You know Mr. Devlin?"

"Know him well," Sergeant Sturdy said genially. "I've kept the boys on patrol out there as I promised. But I guess Mrs. Stoddard didn't think I planned to send them often enough."

"She had a bad fright," Victoria said.

"Sure," the sergeant said. "It's a nasty business. We thought maybe those two had hit it out for Boston some way and then there were those robberies today."

"Robberies?" she raised her eyebrows.

"Two of them," he said. "Both farmhouses on Crane Road. That started the rumpus all over. I guess Mooney and Nora are still with us."

Burke said, "It's not all that big a country. I can't see why you haven't caught up with them."

Sergeant Sturdy looked unhappy. "You'd be surprised how tough some of this countryside is," he said. "We've got a lot more dense woodland around here than most people guess."

"I suppose that is so," Burke admitted.

Victoria gave him an ironic glance and then looked up at Sergeant Sturdy. "I agree. Think of that big forest just back of Collinwood—the one that touches on the Collinwood private cemetery."

"Funny you should mention that, Miss Winters. We've had our eyes on that very area. Some of our men skimmed through it today but it's something like looking for a needle in a haystack. Mooney and the girl could still be hiding there."

"Sounds a likely place," Burke said.

"What sort of person is Mooney?" Victoria asked.

"Not stable," the policeman said. "I'd call him crazy by this time. He's been drinking a lot, taking drugs and all that. The hippies picked him up as a novelty and made a kind of living folk legend of him. That's how the girl got mixed up in this. But they say she's no angel either."

"You think Mooney capable of any kind of violence, then?" Burke said.

Sergeant Sturdy nodded. "He sure wrecked his jail cell before he got out. He has the strength of about three ordinary men and he doesn't care much how he uses it. The thing to do if you see him is run and notify the police."

Victoria smiled ruefully. "If you have the time."

"That does count," the sergeant agreed.

She asked, "What about the robberies? What did they take?"

"Food and some clothing," he said. "Guess Mooney couldn't find anything to fit him at the first place so they tried another. He was luckier next time. The man who owns the farm is big, but not as big as Mooney. Anyway, they took his plaid jacket and a couple of pairs of trousers and some boots."

"What about the girl?" she wanted to know.

The policeman chuckled. "She got a few things, some dresses and underclothes. I reckon it's fairly cold out there these nights and she needed them." He paused. "The funny thing is she left something behind that was worth a lot more than what she took."

"What?" Victoria asked.

"An earring," Sergeant Sturdy said. "I guess you'd be interested in that. I didn't pay much attention to it at first. Found it on the floor of the kitchen of one of the farmhouses. It looked pretty, but that was all. When I went home I showed it to my wife and she figured it was real gold and maybe pretty old. So I took it into the jeweler in Ellsworth for an appraisal."

Victoria was quickly divorced from the noisy surroundings as the old chill of terror suddenly crept through her. "What did he say?"

"Well, he sure surprised me," Sergeant Sturdy admitted sheepishly. "He got pretty excited about that little old earring. Told me it was solid gold and the kind that isn't around much anymore. He claimed it was an antique, maybe more than a hundred years old. And worth plenty!" Victoria sat back as the words burned into her mind. Accidentally she'd been offered another bit of evidence that they were dealing with zombies. Who more likely to own a solid gold earring a century old than Esther Collins?

Burke was quick to sense what she was thinking. She could tell by the troubled expression on his handsome face. Now he turned to Sergeant Sturdy and hurriedly said, "There should be no great mystery about that. She's probably been thieving around and picked the earring up somewhere."

"That's the way I see it," the sergeant agreed. "But I sure think it's funny she should have left something worth a good many times what they took."

"You're right," Burke agreed lamely as he watched Victoria for her reaction.

Sergeant Sturdy nodded brightly. "Well, I must be moving on, folks. Let me know if you see anything suspicious." And he left them to stride down the length of the lounge again and out.

Victoria took a deep breath. "Now what do you say?"

Burke Devlin smiled ruefully. "I know. You're going to tell me that was Esther's earring and she lost it when she and Derek were plundering the farm. I won't go for it."

"I wish you would consider it seriously," she said. "I'd like to go home now. It's getting late."

Not even his goodnight kiss cheered her. The talk with Sergeant Sturdy had heightened her fears that the soulless bodies of Derek and Esther Collins had been freed to bring horror to them all.

She made her way up the dimly lit stairway lost in troubled thoughts. She paused inside the door of her room to turn on the light switch. Before she could touch it, she heard a heavy breathing close to her and then a giant shadow moved in the semi-darkness of the room. Before she could scream, her throat was gripped by large, powerful hands that tightened around her throat until her breath was shut off.

CHAPTER 6

Victoria knew that it was only a matter of seconds before she must surely lose consciousness. The unrelenting pressure tightened on her throat and then she heard Elizabeth's voice from the corridor outside. The knowledge that help was so near gave her the strength to struggle against the horror that was overpowering her.

Elizabeth called out anxiously from the other side of the door, "Victoria, was that you I heard just now? Are you in there?"

She clawed at the thing which was slowly suffocating her, ripped at the hairy hands—but the giant's grip never slackened. In a frantic effort to attract Elizabeth's attention she kicked her heels against the hardwood floor and hoped she was making enough noise to be heard.

Apparently it worked. Elizabeth cried, "Victoria, what's wrong? Answer me!" And there was the sound of the door handle being turned and then the door was flung open and the dim light from the hallway streamed in.

The giant that was throttling her gave an angry grunt and let her fall free to the floor. At the same instant she heard Elizabeth's scream of sheer terror and then the scuffle of retreating footsteps. She lay on her side on the hardwood floor, her hand at her aching throat, fighting hard to remain conscious.

Elizabeth was bending over her. "Victoria, are you all right?"

She nodded and feebly lifted herself on an elbow. "I think so," she whispered hoarsely. "My throat!"

"I know," the older woman said, horror in her voice. "You were very nearly strangled. And that awful man has gotten away."

Elizabeth rose and left her to hurry down the stairs. Victoria could hear the excited voices of Roger and his sister mingling as they compared notes and then Carolyn's anxious tones joined them. Victoria rose unsteadily to her feet. She made her way across to the light switch and turned it on. The room was a shambles. The intruder had ransacked her dresser, leaving most of its contents on the floor. The things hanging in her closet had been tossed this way and that. She was still standing there weakly surveying the damage when Elizabeth rejoined her along with Roger and Carolyn. The three stared at the disorder in astonishment.

Roger spoke first. "What was he looking for?"

"He must have wanted something badly to cause all that havoc," Carolyn commented.

Elizabeth was frowning. "Or else he's just plain out of his mind. Why else would he wait here in the dark and attack Victoria?"

"How did he get in?" Roger demanded. "I assume all the doors were locked."

"I don't know," Elizabeth admitted. "He left by the front entrance. The door was wide open when I went down."

"He might have come in through the side cellar door," Carolyn suggested. "I know it has no lock."

"It's usually kept bolted on the inside," Roger said irritably. "And even if it wasn't, how would he know about it? And how was he able to find his way into the main part of the house and up here without anyone hearing?"

"We were all in our rooms. It wouldn't be difficult," Elizabeth said.

"If he knew the house," Roger reminded her. "And I don't see how he could have." He glanced at Victoria. "I think that girl should have a good drink of brandy."

Elizabeth nodded and told Carolyn, "Go down and get the brandy, dear."

The girl looked toward the stairs apprehensively. "I don't like to go alone."

"It's all right," Elizabeth promised. "The front door is locked and there is no one in the house but us. So be a good girl and do as I say." With some reluctance Carolyn left to get the brandy.

"You look as if you might faint," Roger said worriedly, taking her arm to guide her to a chair.

"I'll be alright," Victoria promised weakly as she sat down. She was only now beginning to think what it could mean. Naturally the others were assuming the intruder was Tim Mooney, the escaped killer. But she was convinced it was Derek Collins who had upset her room and then attacked her. For some reason the zombie had been drawn to that room, had expected to find something there. She was sure that Derek Collins was familiar with all the secrets of the old mansion.

Roger interrupted her thoughts by asking his sister, "Did you get a good look at the fellow?"

Elizabeth paused in her straightening up of the dresser to turn and tell him, "Yes. It was the same terrible looking creature that tried to wave down my car the other night. It was Mooney! I'm certain of it. And hadn't you better phone Sergeant Sturdy and let him know Mooney has been here?"

Roger nodded. "I'll do that right away." He passed Carolyn arriving with the brandy as he went out and called back, "See that Victoria gets some of that brandy right away."

Carolyn poured her a generous glass and handed it to her. Victoria took several sips of the strong, biting liquor and it helped her throat.

Carolyn glanced at her with concern. "Shouldn't we call a doctor?"

"No. I'm going to be alright," Victoria said in an almost normal voice. "My throat has improved a lot already and this is helping."

Elizabeth had retrieved most of the things scattered on the floor by the dresser. She shook her head. "I just don't understand it," she said. "He must be insane."

After a few minutes Roger came back upstairs. "I talked with Sturdy," he said in a disgruntled voice. "He wants to come right over. I couldn't get him to wait until morning. So I don't imagine we'll get any sleep."

"I think it's right he should come at once," Elizabeth told her brother. "Victoria could have been killed. And Mooney did break into the house. It's a serious business. They may manage to pick him up on the grounds."

"I doubt that," Roger said in an irritated tone. "At least David hasn't wakened."

"That boy sleeps like a log," Elizabeth said thankfully. "I only hope the sergeant doesn't arrive with a screaming siren to announce him. That would wake him."

"It's not likely he'd do that," Carolyn said. "It would warn Mooney if he's hiding out there somewhere."

"Don't be too sure," Roger commented. "You feel well enough to stay up and answer the police questions?" he asked Victoria.

"Yes," she said.

Sergeant Sturdy arrived within fifteen minutes and came

straight up to question her and Elizabeth about the incident, since they were the only ones in the house who had actually seen the intruder. He took notes and seemed especially interested in what Mooney had on.

"I can't tell you," Victoria confessed. "He attacked me in the darkness. I saw nothing more than his shadow."

The heavyset man turned to Elizabeth. "What about you, Mrs. Stoddard? You must have gotten a good look at him."

"Not really," the older woman said. "He gave me such a shock. And then he brushed by me—really, threw me back so I wouldn't bar his way. I don't think I could tell you what he was wearing. Whatever it was didn't stand out or impress me."

"Maybe a plaid jacket and dark trousers?" the Sergeant suggested.

"Perhaps so," Elizabeth said shakily. "I honestly can't say."

"But you did recognize him as the man who tried to stop you on the road?"

"Yes. He had the same long black hair. And that strange look in his eyes—an almost expressionless stare. And he was a giant."

"It fits," the policeman said, gazing about the room. "You say he messed everything up in here?"

"Yes," Victoria said. "Mrs. Stoddard has put a good deal of it to rights."

The sergeant looked glum as he glanced at Elizabeth. "I wish you hadn't done that," he told her. "You should have left everything as it was."

The dark woman looked mildly surprised. "I can't imagine why! It isn't as if a murder had been committed or anything like that. What possible help could it have been to have seen the things strewn all over the place?"

"That's exactly what I don't know," he said in a weary tone. "In our business we like to see everything just as it's been left. Often the entire picture suggests something that part of it doesn't."

Elizabeth frowned. "I'm sorry. I was trying to help. And shouldn't you be searching the grounds for Mooney instead of being here questioning us?"

Sergeant Sturdy gave her an annoyed glance. "My men are doing that, ma'am." He put his notebook back in his pocket. "Well, I guess that will be all for now. You want to be sure the doors are all locked or bolted in future. It looks as if he came in through that cellar entrance."

"We'll take care of that," Roger promised. "And you'll be keeping an eye out for him in the immediate area?"

"I'm sending an extra man over," the sergeant promised. When the others started out, Sergeant Sturdy hung back a moment to speak to Victoria alone as she stood in the doorway watching them leave. "If you remember anything else I wish you'd get in touch with me."

"I'll be glad to," she faltered.

His stem eyes met hers. "There's something about the way you told your story that makes me think you're holding something back."

Her eyes widened with surprise. "Why do you say that?"

"A hunch," he told her as he continued staring at her.

"You're wrong," she said awkwardly. "I've told you all I know."

"Think it over," he told her. "You can always get me at my office." And with that he turned and followed the others downstairs.

For a moment she was tempted to call him back and confess her true fears. But she waited long enough for him to get out of sight and then she began to feel that he'd only scoff at her theories anyway. Of course she could take him to the cemetery and show him the shattered coffins, but he'd probably agree with Burke Devlin about that.

She closed the door and sat on her bed. There was nothing to do now but wait for further developments. It was bad to have the sergeant suspicious of her, especially when she felt unable to confide in him. As soon as possible she wanted to tell Burke what had happened and talk it over with him.

Some things puzzled her. Why had the zombie visited her room, if a zombie it had been? Did Derek Collins blame her and Burke Devlin for interfering with the tomb? Could she expect further attacks by the living dead man? Or were the others right in assuming the intruder had been Tim Mooney? This confusion of questions racked her mind long after she'd gone to bed.

The next morning she phoned Burke at the hotel. She gave him the bare details of what had happened, ending with, "The sergeant seemed to think I might be holding back some information."

"Were you?"

"Only that I think it was Derek Collins in my room."

"Do you think the police will listen to your zombie story?"

"No. That's why I didn't tell the sergeant."

"That showed some judgment," he told her. "You've got to be extra careful until the police pick up Mooney and that girl. He was probably looking for clothes for her and money."

"Then why pick my room?" she said. "It's not the easiest one to reach and I haven't much in the way of clothes or money to steal."

"Coincidence," Burke said tersely.

"We've too much of that as it is," Victoria warned him. "I'm sure there's more to it than that."

"Such as?"

"I don't know," she said, hesitating. "Perhaps because we interfered with his tomb or maybe it has something to do with the history of the house that I am not familiar with."

"Get those thoughts out of your mind," he insisted in a worried tone. "And take care of yourself. I'm going to have to be away for a few days and I don't care to spend all my time wondering if you're alright."

"I'll manage," she promised.

"Not by the sound of last night," he said. "I'll be in touch with you as soon as I get back."

After she put down the phone she spent an hour or so with David in the study. When she had him occupied with a series of arithmetic tests she left him and went out to the kitchen to see Elizabeth, whom she found seated at the kitchen table studying a cookbook.

"I'm trying to find a new dessert for dinner. Both David and Carolyn have been complaining." She gave her an appraising glance. "You look much better. Is your throat bothering you?"

"Just the bruises," Victoria said. "I'd almost forgotten about it."

"Well, I haven't," her employer promised. "I intend to keep after the police until they clear up this mystery. Otherwise we won't ever have a minute's peace."

"If they *can* clear it up," Victoria said pointedly.

"Oh, I'm certain they will," the older woman said. "I listened to the news this morning. Several people saw Mooney and the girl last night."

"Were they seen near here?"

Elizabeth frowned. "No. That's a little baffling, isn't it? All the reports placed them about ten miles away."

Once again Victoria felt herself tense with fear and doubt. The reports backed up her zombie theory. They would probably worry Sergeant Sturdy. She wondered what he'd make of them.

"But then," Elizabeth said, "you can't put much stock in the stories. Some people will say anything just to get attention. They may never have seen the criminals at all but merely pretended to. Or they may have seen a shadow and decided it was Mooney. We know that he was here."

"I suppose that is so," Victoria said reluctantly. Abruptly she changed the conversation to something which interested her a good deal more. "I've been wondering," she said. "Do you have a really authentic history of the family?"

Elizabeth seemed mildly surprised at her question. "No. I don't believe so," she said. "There is a brief account by Grandfather Collins, but Roger has it in the library in his office."

"I see," Victoria said. "I've been studying some of the portraits and I'd like to know more about the people they depict—such as Derek Collins, for instance."

The older woman shut the cookbook and frowned. "Derek Collins! He was a bad one. I don't know if I remember anything more than I already told you—that Derek was in the slave trade, and had a fine vessel, the *Mary Dorn*, but something dreadful happened aboard her during a visit to Barbados. Derek Collins never returned from that voyage alive, nor did his wife Esther."

"And you never heard what happened?" Victoria asked pointedly.

"No," Elizabeth said. "I couldn't get my grandfather to talk about it. I think there must have been a double murder. According to the family records it was right after that Derek and his young bride were brought here for burial."

"Then they were buried here," Victoria prodded gently.

Elizabeth nodded. "Yes. My grandfather often told of a waiting crowd at the Collinsport wharf when the *Mary Dorn* returned. No one had heard about the tragedy. News traveled slowly in those days and the late mail was aboard the vessel. When she docked, the first mate revealed what had happened and the coffins containing the bodies were carried from the ship."

"And that was all anyone ever saw of them?" Victoria asked, trying to find out whether the coffins had been opened and the bodies seen on their arrival.

"Derek's parents never set eyes on him again," Elizabeth said with a sigh. "Grandfather was always mysterious at this point but he said, because of something in a letter from Esther Collins' father, the family had stout oaken cases made to cover the mahogany caskets."

"I wonder why?"

"I don't know. It's so long since I heard the story I'm foggy on a lot of the details," the older woman admitted. "Derek and his young bride were put in that vault you've seen in our cemetery. And the *Mary Dorn* was sold and never came back to Maine again. She was sunk in a hurricane on her way to South America several years later. The family weren't surprised. They always spoke of her as being a cursed ship."

"It's an interesting story," Victoria said. "Thanks for telling it to me."

Elizabeth rose from the table with a smile. "I'll speak to Roger if you like and ask him to bring that small history home so you can read it."

"I wouldn't want to trouble him," she said.

"He won't mind," Elizabeth promised. "I'll mention it to him."

Victoria left the older woman with few answers to the problems that were tormenting her. Yet she had found out one thing. The coffins had not been opened on their arrival in Collinsport. This supported Burke Devlin's theory that the bodies had never left the West Indies, that only weighted caskets with the mummified frog in them had been sent back. In which case she had no need to fear they'd been instrumental in releasing the zombies.

But Burke could be wrong. Even though the caskets had not been opened, this did not necessarily mean there were no bodies in them. There were a number of reasons for not viewing the bodies— including the crude embalming available and the long passage of time on a voyage through warm seas. Not to mention the most significant fact; the distraught father-in-law had taken the trouble to write a special letter which resulted in Derek's father securing those outer oaken cases and placing the coffins in them.

Victoria stopped still in the corridor as the pieces fitted in her mind. It had to mean that the family had been warned of the zombie treatment given to the bodies. And to guard against the voodoo threat they had followed instructions and interred them in a special way. So they must have been certain the bodies were in the caskets.

Because David was still busy with the arithmetic tests she spent only a moment or two with him. Then she went on to the living room, her thoughts racing as she considered all the evil possibilities with which she might be faced. She wished that Burke was not going away. Although they disagreed on this matter, she was at least able to discuss it with him. Now she would be alone with her fears. There was no one she could confide in unless she tried to explain it all to Sergeant Sturdy. And she was willing to agree with Burke in this—the sergeant would never believe her.

Now she stood in the great living room with its heavy drapes, antique furniture and rich carpets and studied the portrait of the century dead Derek. The mocking eyes seemed to taunt her and the cruel lips gave the suggestion of being twisted in a sneer. Was this the giant who had tried to kill her last night? Was a zombie Derek lurking somewhere in the shadows of the forest now waiting only for night to come after her again?

As she asked herself these questions she had a sudden inspiration. She need not be alone in her dilemma. She had Amos Martin to turn to and if she used the short cut to the beach road and went down to his place before dark there would be little risk involved. This decision made, she hurried from the living room and went back to check the answers to David's test in the study.

By three thirty she was free to go to Amos Martin's. Elizabeth had driven to Ellsworth on business and Carolyn had been given permission to use the station wagon for the afternoon. So Carolyn and David had gone into Collinsport for an hour. There was no one left at the sprawling dark mansion but the surly Matt Morgan, the handyman. As a rule Victoria saw little of him.

As it was a dull, cool afternoon she threw a trench coat over her shoulders before starting down the narrow path that skirted the cliff and took her quickly to the beach road. From that point it was only a fifteen minutes' walk to Amos Martin's battered house. Large white gulls circled overhead and uttered their harsh cries as she made her way down the steep incline. The ocean had a drab, gray look, but there was no wind and it was smooth enough.

The beach road, like the private road to Collinwood, had little traffic, and it had fallen into a bad state of repair. Grass grew here and there through its gravel surface and there were plenty of ruts in it. Its shoulders were washed away dangerously in many places. The monotonous dirge of the waves on the beach followed her as she hurried towards the weatherbeaten house.

As she drew near it she saw the spare figure of Amos Martin standing before it. He seemed to be staring out at the ocean, unaware of her approach. The old man was perfectly motionless and even when she came up beside him the emaciated, eagle face showed no expression nor did he turn his head. He wore a battered soft hat with only the suggestion of a crease in it and the rest of his clothing, including the bedraggled black sweater that was his protection against the cool of the afternoon, was shabby and shapeless.

"Mr. Martin," she said eagerly.

Only then did he turn and study her with his sunken, rheumy eyes. "You are the believer," he said in his raspy voice.

"Yes. I was here the other day with Burke Devlin."

He nodded. "We talked with my Ma. She has come to me with a warning since then. There is a shadow over Collinwood." He paused. "A shadow over you!"

"That's why I came to talk to you," she said. "Burke is away and I have no one else."

He stood there watching her with those glazed eyes, the emaciated face giving no hint of expression. "You have released them," he said. "I know. I have seen them more than once."

Her brow furrowed. "You really think there are zombies? That Derek and Esther are at large?"

"They have been on the beach," he said. "And last night she peered in my window. I saw her white face pressed against the glass and her staring eyes. And I guess that he was not far off. Those two, they stay together. But I raised a hand and made the sign of the cross and she vanished." Victoria didn't know whether to believe him or not. Burke had warned her that Amos knew all the techniques of the professional spiritualists. He might be telling her this to frighten her and bend her to his will, or it might be merely the fancy of a weary old brain. It was more charitable to think that. But suppose he were telling the truth?

With a tiny shiver she drew the trench coat around her shoulders and asked, "Did the sign of the cross send her away?"

"Aye," he said solemnly. "She is a creature of the devil."

Victoria was anxious to tell her own story. She said, "Last night someone in my room attacked me. Tried to choke me. He was waiting for me when I came in. I couldn't see his face but he was a giant and strong!"

"Derek Collins," the old man said in his rasping voice. "You think so?"

"Aye."

"But why attack me? Why come to my room?"

"What room do you have, girl?" Amos Martin asked her.

She told where it was located on the third floor. She ended with, "The people at Collinwood think it was Tim Mooney who came into the house to rob it. But I can't believe it. Why should he skip all the other rooms and come to mine?"

"It was Derek," Amos said. "You are in the very room that once was his."

This really startled her. "How can you be sure?"

"I know. I heard it long ago. So he was only coming back to his own. It was you were the intruder," Amos declared.

It was the first logical explanation she'd had for the giant being in her room and yet it would be far from logical as far as the others were concerned. She looked up at the old man imploringly. "Amos, don't tell me a thing like that unless you are sure it is so," she said. "I'm frightened half out of my mind!"

The old man nodded. "It is the room Derek had before he sailed on the *Mary Dorn*. And now he is back from the dead and wants it."

"What am I going to do?" she cried.

"Elizabeth frightened him away. It is not likely you will see him again."

"But if there really are such things as zombies and Burke and I have freed them to terrorize these people, they should be warned," she said agitatedly. "Don't you think I ought to tell them?"

Something like a sneering smile twisted the gaping black mouth and he chuckled hoarsely. "You try to tell them and they will call you daft as they do me."

"You think so?"

"Aye."

"But what can I do?"

"Take care for yourself and wait until the zombies come to some harm," the old man said. "They cannot survive fire. Eventually the flame will find them and they will return to the hell from whence they've journeyed."

Victoria gave a deep sigh. "I must go back."

"Wait!" The old man raised a skinny hand. "Come with me!"

Somewhat dubiously she followed him as with a shaky step he led her toward the rear door of the old house. When she went inside she was met by the same disorder and stale smell of leftover food as on the other occasions when she'd been there. Using the furniture for support, he leaned first on a chair back, then the edge of the table and then another chair back as he made his way across the crowded, shadowed kitchen. When he reached a high cupboard he fumbled with a bony hand until he had the door opened. Then he rummaged on its shelf and drew out something.

He turned to her and with a triumphant air offered her a small wooden crucifix. "Take that," he said in his harsh voice. "It will protect you better than any weapon."

She accepted it reluctantly. "I don't want to rob you of it."

The sunken eyes met hers. "You can pay me one day if it serves you well."

Victoria recalled Burke's warning that the old man was preying on her fears for profit. Yet she was in no position to turn down any offer of help. She put the crucifix in her pocket and said, "Thanks."

Because she wanted to be back at Collinwood before the others, she left the old man and hurried back along the beach road to the path leading up the cliffs. It seemed even lonelier than before. The ocean offered its usual melancholy sound and the gulls their harsh, angry cries. She had almost reached the bottom of the path when the strange wave of fear struck her. She was so suddenly filled with terror that she stopped still.

It was then she felt the presence behind her. She heard nothing but the waves and gulls; there was no warning sound, but she knew someone was there close to her. Someone whose eyes were upon her. Slowly she glanced over her shoulder and standing in plain view on the beach road was the mad-looking giant of a man.

She gave a sharp cry of fear and stumbled back. The giant with staring eyes and long black hair came toward her with a weaving, strange walk. She screamed again and began to stumble up the steep path. And now she could hear him behind her, his heavy breathing as he came close and his footsteps on the rocks.

Victoria raced up the steep incline sobbing with fear, her chest paining from exertion and knowing that the thing behind her was catching up with her. She fell over a heavy stone and with an instinct born of desperation, dived down to lift it high in her hands and dash it back toward her pursuer. It found its mark for she heard a roar of pain and he did not come forward. She resumed her flight to the top of the cliff, every step becoming more difficult as she reached the top. And then gazing down at her, directly in her path, she saw a girl with flowing yellow hair and staring eyes. The girl was waiting for her!

CHAPTER 7

Panting heavily, Victoria halted and she stared in terror at the weird girl blocking her way. At any moment the giant whose progress she had temporarily stopped would be coming after her once more. She was caught between these two demons—these creatures from hell, as Amos Martin had termed them. And with that she remembered the crucifix he had given her.

She whipped it out of her coat pocket and held it high so the yellow-haired girl could not help seeing it. The crucifix had an immediate effect on the strange creature. Her face twisted in a tormented fashion and she gave a hoarse cry and moved back in a crouching fashion. She vanished in the bushes and Victoria went on up to the top of the cliff.

As she reached level ground she saw Carolyn and David walking across the field to meet her. Concerned for their safety, she hurried towards them. Once she glanced back and saw no sign of the frightening duo who had almost trapped her on the path. And she thought she knew what had happened. They would not show themselves now that more than one person was in the area. At the approach of David and Carolyn they had hidden themselves in the bushes—another hint that Burke Devlin might be right and they were dealing with criminals on the run rather than the terrifying creations of a voodoo witch doctor.

David came forward to greet her. "Matt told us you had walked toward the cliff. We thought you must have taken the path to the beach."

"I did," she said, managing a smile in spite of her shaken condition. "I'm glad you came to meet me." It was, she thought, a masterpiece of understatement.

Carolyn asked, "Did you have a nice walk?"

"It was a change," Victoria told her guardedly.

"I must go down some afternoon," the other girl said.

"It's lonely," Victoria warned her. "You should always take someone with you."

"You didn't," Carolyn pointed out.

"I should have," Victoria said. "And I will if I go again."

"Take me with you," David said as they strolled back toward Collinwood. "I'll protect you."

"Thanks for the offer," Victoria said with a smile. "I'll be sure to remember it."

Carolyn gave her a forlorn look. "I saw Joe in town and he wanted to take me out tonight. I had to tell him no. I explained that mother wouldn't let me go out at night until they'd caught those two."

"I'm sure he wouldn't want to put you in danger," Victoria said.

The other girl lowered her head and scuffed the ground sulkily. "He was mad because I told him I couldn't see him." She gave Victoria a glance. "It seems to me I'm in as much danger at home—that Tim Mooney might show up here again and I might be the victim next time."

"I hardly think he'll dare come back," Victoria said.

"I wish he would," David enthused.

"You wouldn't if you met up with him," Carolyn warned. "And anyway you're not supposed to be listening to our talk."

"You're just sore because you can't see Joe!" David taunted her. Laughing, he ran on ahead of them towards the house.

"He can be mean when he likes," Carolyn said angrily. "First thing I know Joe will be finding himself another girl."

"I'm sure he's much too fond of you," Victoria told her. "And don't worry so. This trouble will soon be all settled."

"I wish I could believe that!" Carolyn said mournfully.

Elizabeth arrived back from Ellsworth in time to join them at the dinner table. She looked tired and at once began to tell about her adventures. "What a dreadful day," she said. "I went to talk with Simon Blair's lawyers in Ellsworth. They tried to urge the old man to sell me his property, but he wouldn't listen."

Roger smiled nastily from his end of the table. "I won't say I told you so."

"I know you did," Elizabeth agreed calmly. "I suppose it was too much to hope that Simon Blair would talk business, the way his mind is buried in the past."

"What's he like, Mother?" Carolyn asked. "Is he really ancient, like Amos Martin?"

"He's neither as old nor frail as Amos," Elizabeth said. "But he has a nasty stubborn streak. And a vicious tongue. He's determined to keep that feud going. He said he wouldn't sell his property to a family whose wealth was built on the profits of the slave trade."

"Sounds like him!" Roger agreed.

"And it simply isn't true," his sister complained. "Most of our money has been made here in the fish-packing plant. When the sailing ships were replaced by steamships our family lost a great deal of money. They never regained it until they opened the packing plant."

"You should have told him so," Carolyn said indignantly.

"I suppose I should have," her mother agreed with a touch of weariness. "But I hardly felt up to arguing the family morality back to Derek Collins." She gave Victoria a faint smile. "Simon Blair, like you, has a deep interest in our renegade ancestor."

"He was a colorful character while he lasted," was Roger's opinion. "And that's more than you can say about Simon Blair."

"Blair has promised never to sell us the land while he's alive," Elizabeth said.

"Postpone the expansion until he dies," Carolyn suggested.

"He's a very tough old fellow," Elizabeth told her. "He may live for years."

Victoria listened to it all without making any comment. Her mind was on other matters. She was thinking of the near escape she'd had in the afternoon and that it was only quick thinking and the arrival of David and Carolyn that had saved her from who knew what. She would have to thank Amos Martin for the crucifix next time she visited him. And she meant to try and find out more about voodoo as soon as she could.

After dinner she went into the library and searched for any book that might deal with the subject. While she was there Roger came in to join her. He was in a better mood than usual. Apparently Elizabeth had told him about Victoria wanting to read the family history.

He said, "Hear you are anxious to read the Collins history that Grandfather wrote."

She nodded. "Yes. I'm sure it must be interesting."

Roger winked. "Well, not all the family rogues are of this generation. We had a few black sheep in the family from the beginning. That Derek we mentioned at dinner was a prize one."

"The one in the slave traffic."

"He was in it, all right," Roger asserted. "That's why our family sold off his ship after he died. They wanted no part of the *Mary Dorn*."

"She was supposed to be cursed, wasn't she?" Victoria asked.

He nodded. "That was the story. I guess it began with all that happened aboard that night in Barbados. It wound up with Derek and his wife dead. There was a lot of voodoo mixed up in it, according to legend."

"Voodoo and Maine," she said. "They don't seem to go together."

"From time to time they've been linked more closely than you'd guess," Roger said. "All our ships plied trade with the West Indies. The sailors were bound to learn the lore of the islands. As a boy I remember hearing my grandfather tell about his grandparent explaining the meaning of the voodoo drums—the Rada drums of the dark forest. The talking drum played only with the hands, the second drum and the third. The natives used them to invoke the gods, both good and bad. One was the Loa Azoua, whose touch brought you a wound or sore that would not heal. The white men from Maine learned to respect the black man's magic and beware of it."

"And you say the deaths of this Derek and his wife were brought about by voodoo?"

He frowned. "Not exactly. But voodoo was mixed up in it. So long ago the whole business is vague. My grandfather didn't like to talk about it."

That was all she learned directly from Roger. He seemed to have almost the same information concerning the *Mary Dorn* and her renegade captain as Elizabeth. They had both been told essentially the same story. She waited for Roger to bring her the family history as he'd promised, but he kept putting it off and she despaired of ever seeing it.

Meanwhile the days passed and Burke had not yet returned. Mooney and Nora remained at large. The general opinion was that they had somehow escaped the ring the police had thrown around the Collinsport area and vanished in Boston or one of the other cities. Here they would find shelter with some of the hippies who admired Mooney so much.

Tension eased and things returned to normal. The several visits of the patrol car each day were discontinued and Elizabeth even agreed to allow Carolyn an occasional evening date with Joe again. Victoria began to believe that Burke had been right.

The fantasies in her mind concerning the zombies were probably no more than that. She had been wrong to let Amos Martin alarm her with his weird story of the living dead. And the bodies of Derek and Esther had probably disintegrated long ago somewhere in far away Barbados. She began to feel the whole experience had been a dreadful nightmare.

But there was one person in the area who appeared to be still concerned. And that was Sergeant Sturdy. He made a special trip out to Collinwood one sunny June afternoon to talk to her. He suggested they take a stroll on the grounds for privacy.

When they were walking along the path by the cliffs, he said, "I came by to see if you'd remembered anything more to tell me."

She looked at him in amazement. "About what?"

His weatherbeaten face was stern. "About the night you were nearly strangled. About all that has gone on here."

"But Tim Mooney and that girl have gone. Everyone says so."

He eyed her sharply. "What do you say?"

She shrugged. "The same, I guess."

The path where they were walking was close to the edge of the cliff. He halted and staring at her, said, "But you know more than they do."

She was perplexed and troubled. "Why do you say that?"

"Because I guessed it from your manner that other night."

"You were wrong."

"I'm never wrong about things like that," Sergeant Sturdy told her confidently. "Now you can tell me or you can refuse. If you refuse you may be sorry."

"How can I be sorry about something I don't know?" she said evasively. The business of the zombies was of the past now. She had no intention of trying to explain what she'd feared when they seemed a real threat. It would only make her look ridiculous.

"I see," he said. "You're still determined to keep it to yourself."

"I have nothing to tell you," she insisted stubbornly.

"The same thing," he told her as they resumed walking along Widow's Hill. "Now I think this lull we're having is going to come to an end one day soon. And very soon! The area will be alive with rumors again and you'll be partly to blame for not being frank with me now."

"If I knew anything that would help I'd tell you," she said. "Please believe that."

He regarded her soberly. "I think you're trying to be honest with me. But you just don't understand," he said. "And when you do it may be too late."

"Tim Mooney and Nora are in Boston," she said. "Or that's what I've heard. Why don't the police find them there?"

"That's an interesting question," he agreed. "And I was hoping you might help us find an answer."

"I'm sorry," she said. "I can't help you."

"I see," he said with a sigh. "No use walking any further then." They headed back to Collinwood. Before he got into his car to leave he told her, "I'll be back one day."

The visit of the police officer brought back some of her old fears and left her filled with grim forebodings. Sergeant Sturdy, because of his long experience in police work, had acquired a sensitivity to false notes in the testimony of a witness. And so he had known that night he questioned her that she had only told him part of what was keeping her in fear. And he wanted the full truth.

But he didn't guess how fantastic the full truth was. She couldn't imagine the down-to-earth sergeant seriously listening to her theory that it was the living dead who were creating havoc around Collinsport. He mistakenly thought she had additional information on the doings of Tim Mooney and his girl. And he seemed convinced they would turn up again. She felt the chances were all against this happening.

Burke came home the first of the following week. And he at once phoned her and invited her to have dinner with him at the hotel that night. He didn't pick her up himself, as he was trying to catch up with paperwork that had accumulated during his absence. One of his men came with the convertible and drove her into the village. But Burke was waiting in the hotel lobby to greet her.

He planted a quick kiss on her lips and said, "Sorry I wasn't able to go out for you. Just too much to do here. And I've been wanting to ask you at least a thousand questions."

She laughed. "Don't expect me to provide anything like that many answers."

Their serious discussion began over the dinner table. In a quiet corner of the softly lighted dining room Burke Devlin began discussing the disappearance of Mooney and Nora. He said, "You may as well admit it. With Mooney and the girl gone your zombies have vanished as well."

"I'm almost convinced," she said. "Yet I can't forget that experience on the cliff when I found myself trapped between them."

"It was Mooney chasing you. And Nora who stood in your way. It wasn't Martin's crucifix that terrified her, it was the approach of David and Carolyn. You couldn't see them from where you were on the cliff."

"You always manage to sound convincing," she said defensively.

He smiled. "Admit you were wrong."

"I'd rather wait awhile," she said.

"Whatever you say," he said, generously. "You needn't worry anymore about Derek and Esther Collins."

"I'm glad you're back," she said. "I've missed you."

"That's important to me," he said, his eyes gentle as they met hers.

"It seemed there was no one to talk to. No one I could trust."

"I intended to get back sooner," Burke said. "But things kept delaying me. At least you did go down to see Amos that day."

"Which was a mistake. I nearly got in trouble."

"I agree," he said. "And I think once Amos saw how seriously you took his story he built on it. He deliberately played on your fears."

"That was cruel of him!"

"He's an odd old man who is past thinking of anything but himself and his strange nightmares. He saw a chance to impress you and get money from you."

"You don't think he believes in any of the things he claims to?"

"I don't think he's the devoted disciple of spiritualism he pretends," Burke Devlin said acidly. "He saw too much of his mother's dealings in the spirits for that. Still, he may believe in some of it."

"You were the one who first took me to see him."

Burke smiled. "Because you were such a skeptic at that time. You soon caught up and overtook me."

"We must go back to Amos Martin's," she said. "I want to return his crucifix and give him something for his trouble."

"Tomorrow night, if I can manage it," he promised. "There doesn't seem to be any talk about Mooney in the village. I guess it's a dead subject. He's slipped away from them and is hiding out somewhere."

"Sergeant Sturdy thinks he'll come back."

"Sergeant Sturdy is a born pessimist," Burke Devlin joked. "I wouldn't pay any attention to what he says."

"I wonder," she said.

The following day Roger surprised her by bringing home the leather-bound family history written in a fine, neat hand by his grandfather. The ink had faded to a dull brown, but all the entries were clear and easily readable. As soon as she had a moment she sat down with it. The early pages were interesting, but not what she was especially concerned with. She flipped the pages of the old man's journal until she came to the heading bearing Derek Collins' name. The item was not long but she read it with avid excitement.

The old man got right to the point. "Derek Collins proved a great disappointment and source of trouble to his worthy father. A giant of a young man, he seemed a likely candidate for a glorious career. And, indeed, his natural talents and vigor would have made this easy for him. It was said of him that he had the bodily strength of three ordinary men and he stood well above six feet. His father sent him to sea and in due time made him captain of his own ship, the *Mary Dorn*. Never was a plan to go more miserably awry. Young Captain Derek became known as a rake and spendthrift in every port he touched. He gambled away the ship's profits and went heavily in debt.

"To recoup his fortunes and prevent censure from his father

when he returned to Maine, he decided to make one voyage with the *Mary Dorn* as a slaver. But the profit from this black gold was so excellent and the money slipped through his fingers so easily he enlisted in the vicious trade and made it his sole business. It was at this period he wooed and won the daughter of a governor of Barbados. The poor girl was distraught on learning of her husband's occupation. There was a quarrel in which her father was also involved. It ended one night in murder and suicide. The bodies of Derek and Esther Collins were returned to Collinsport and buried here. The *Mary Dorn* was sold, but many of us still believe the voodoo curse that hung over her now shadows Collinwood."

That was all the old man had written. But it was enough. Victoria put the journal down with the feeling that Roger's grandfather had keenly resented the shame and menace brought to Collinwood by the renegade young captain. And without a doubt there had been a long string of misfortunes in the years that had followed. Ernest's untimely death by accident could be thought of as the most recent of these tragic events. And again she was reminded of how much shadow Ernest's death had brought to them all, especially herself.

She made no mention of the journal to Burke when she met him the following evening. As he had promised he would, he took her down to visit Amos Martin. It was a pleasant night and the old man was seated on a bench outside his house when they drove up.

The eagle face brightened when he saw Burke Devlin. "I knew you would be back in time," he said in his feeble rasp.

"In time?" Burke said with a smile. "In time for what?"

"For them to show themselves again," the old man said.

Victoria asked him, "You mean Mooney and his girl?"

The sunken eyes held a cold glitter as they regarded her. "You know well enough who I mean."

"Now wait a minute," Burke challenged him. "You're not going to try telling us those zombies are still around."

"I have seen them."

"You're joking!" Burke said.

"I saw them last night," the old man insisted. "They will show themselves when the moon is full again."

"I think we've heard enough about zombies," Burke said.

"And you will hear more," Amos Martin said and began one of his coughing spells.

When it was over Victoria offered him the crucifix back. "Thank you for letting me have it," she said.

The old man pushed it away with a skinny hand. "No. You will need it!"

She gave Burke a questioning look. He frowned. "Look here," he told the old man, "I think this has gone far enough. You've nothing to gain by trying to frighten Miss Winters anymore."

Amos regarded him calmly. "You will find out when the full moon shows."

Burke turned from him in exasperation and told Victoria, "Let's get away from here." He left the old man five dollars and they got into the convertible and drove off.

She said, "What did you make of all that?"

Burke's voice was angry. "I didn't like it. Amos went beyond the bounds of good taste. We'll not go there again."

"Burke," she said, a note of fear in her voice. "I think he really believes what he said."

"That full moon stuff! Ridiculous! Mooney is somewhere in the hippie jungles of one of the cities. When the police catch up with him that's where they'll find him."

"He was talking about the zombies. He claims the full moon will bring them out once more."

Burke gave her a nervous glance. "Pay no attention to him!"

"I can't help it," she said unhappily. "I think it's true and I'm frightened all over again."

"That's the last time we'll ever see that old man," Burke said angrily. "And let's change the subject. The June Fair is Saturday night and I'm counting on you attending it with me."

"I'd forgotten all about it," she admitted.

"Well, start planning now," he told her. "It's Collinsport's biggest event and we certainly don't want to miss it."

As the week progressed everyone seemed to be of one mind. They all wanted to enjoy Fair Day. It had been a tradition in Collinsport over the years and had not even been discontinued during the days of World War II. The fair was held in a big field outside Collinsport and on the edge of one of the stretches of timberland. Elizabeth was a member of the organizing committee for the first time in many years and was taking a lively interest in the project.

"We're having all kinds of sideshows and rides for the kiddies," she told Victoria. "The Fair Committee is bringing in a traveling carnival for the day. And there'll be the usual cooking contests, cattle judging, turkey dinner and flower show."

Victoria smiled. "Sounds like a lively program."

"It is," the older woman agreed. "We're even having one of those wrestling shows that are so popular. After the match, the chief wrestler will take on all comers."

David and Carolyn were full of plans for the day and the evening that was to follow. And it was decided they would all attend the fair and eat there as well. Only Roger was against the scheme. He preferred to make a quick visit to the fair in the afternoon and then go home to a leisurely dinner. Elizabeth left him plenty of food and told him he could take it from the refrigerator and serve himself.

The grounds were filled with strolling people. The crowd had gathered from as far distant as Portland, Augusta and Bangor and the parking lot was packed with cars. A bandstand had been set up a slight distance from the center of the grounds and the Portland City Band held forth there for a concert in the early part of the evening. They concluded their offerings with "The Stars and Stripes Forever," after which the bandstand was quickly cleared and converted into a wrestling ring.

Victoria was not fond of wrestling, but because Burke Devlin was interested she stood there with him watching the match. When it finally ended, the announcer came to the center of the grandstand to name the winner. His decision was greeted with good-natured cheers mixed with boos. He held his hand up for silence and then told them, "The champ will now take on all comers!"

There was a loud murmur of interest at this and a good deal of joking as onlookers shoved each other forward in mock attempts to get each other to take the challenge to the champ. At last one of the younger men doffed his sports jacket and to a loud burst of cheers and applause climbed up onto the bandstand.

Victoria gave Burke a frightened glance. "He'll be hurt!"

"Don't worry," he laughed. "It's all part of the show. The pro wrestler won't go hard on him. It's just to provide the crowd with some laughs."

As it turned out, Burke was right. The reaction of the Collinsport people was much more intense than it had been to the regular match. They really were rooting for the local youth. But even Victoria could see the professional wrestler was just leading him on.

It was dark now. In keeping with the period styling of the fair, the bandstand was lit up by four torches attached to the four end posts. The brilliantly burning torches casting a flickering orange glow over the ring. She let her eyes lift skyward for a moment and saw that some extra illumination was being provided. There was a full moon.

The roar of the crowd directed her attention back to the ring. The pro wrestler had the local youth on his back in the ring for the required count. Through the boos and cheers the announcer asked for another challenger.

Victoria glanced around her and suddenly on the fringe of the crowd she saw a giant figure with a weird-looking face and long black hair push his way through toward the ring. She tightened her hold on Burke's arm and spoke tensely. "Look!"

"Who's that?" he asked, his eyes now on the strange figure as well.

"It's him," she said. "The one who chased me on the beach!"

"No!" he exclaimed. "It must be Mooney back!" He glanced

around anxiously. "I don't see any of the police around."

The crowd cheered as the big man advanced toward the ring, the set expression of a sleepwalker on his coarse face. He wore a plaid jacket and dark trousers and his hair was long and jet-black. There was laughter and jeering as he ponderously climbed into the ring.

Burke spoke in her ear, "I'm going to try and find the sergeant or some other of the local police."

She gave him a frantic look. "Please don't go!"

"Have to!" he said. "Nobody else seems to realize who it is. I've got to get word to the sergeant." And he pushed off into the crowd and in a moment was lost to sight.

Victoria shivered as much from fear as from the cool darkness. In the ring the giant had pushed away the somewhat startled announcer when he tried to help him with his jacket. And the crowd loved this, howling their delight. The giant was an awesome figure as he faced the pro wrestler in the flickering orange glow of the torches.

But the pro was no coward. He grinned and began working his way around the weird looking big man to get a hold on him. The crowd quieted as tension grew. Victoria could hardly bear to watch and she raised her eyes to the full moon again. Amos Martin had promised the zombies would return when the moon was full. And this surely must be Derek Collins there in the ring!

Her eyes were wide with terror as she watched the two circling each other. And then the giant reached forward and effortlessly caught the surprised pro wrestler in a grip. The crowd roared their approval. The giant continued to hold his opponent rigidly. And sheer horror coursed through Victoria as she realized what was going to happen. The sharp crack of the wrestler's spine snapping in two could be plainly heard by all. The giant then dropped the limp body of the professional wrestler on the floor of the bandstand. A shocked, funeral hush fell over the crowd. The others in the grandstand stood back, frozen with honor, as the giant turned and began to make his way out of the ring.

He swung himself down onto the ground. The onlookers moved back from him as if knowing instinctively this was no ordinary man. Victoria knew they must be thinking him a madman; the truth was too fantastic for their imaginations. The giant was moving away from the ring, and coming nearer to her every second. Only then did she realize he was purposely seeking her out. She backed away with a scream!

CHAPTER 8

Victoria's scream was the signal for a general alarm. All the pent-up emotions of the crowd suddenly were voiced in shouts of outrage and shock. The announcer and the others in the ring came to life and began working over the outstretched form of the professional wrestler. The onlookers divided their attention between the ring and the giant madman who was slowly advancing on her.

She screamed again and retreated. The closest of the onlookers jeered and shouted abuse at the unheeding figure, but none of them seemed willing to venture close to his menacing hulk. Now he was almost within reaching distance of her. She moved back again and at the same instance heard Burke Devlin calling out her name.

Glancing frantically in the direction from which his call had come, she saw him racing toward her, followed closely by Sergeant Sturdy. The police officer raised his gun and fired at the giant. Victoria saw him glare at the sergeant and hesitate, but there was no other sign that the bullet had hit him. Then he wheeled around and hurried off into the darkness toward the refuge of the nearby forest.

Sergeant Sturdy ran after him, firing another shot as he ran. Burke Devlin came over to her and put an arm around her. "Are you all right?"

"Yes," she said weakly. He had caught her on the verge of a faint. She gave him a terrified look. "That thing was coming after me."

"I saw that," he said. Staring grimly into the darkness where the monster and Sergeant Sturdy had both vanished, he added, "Let's hope the sergeant catches up with him."

"I wouldn't count on it," she said in a small voice. And she gave her attention to the ring again, which was now the principal scene of activity. A number of people had clambered up into the bandstand and most of the others had surged close to it.

"He's dead!" A hoarse voice shouted from the bandstand. "Mooney killed him!" There was an answering roar of angry voices that showed the temper of the crowd. All the pleasant gaiety of the summer night had been lost. The hubbub and confusion continued.

"I *knew* he killed him," Victoria told Burke. "He did it as casually as a child might break a toy."

"A terrible business," Burke said, staring at the crowds milling around the bandstand under the yellow glare of the four torches.

"So Amos Martin wasn't so wrong after all."

Burke frowned. "What has Martin to do with this? It simply means that Tim Mooney didn't leave here as we thought. He's been hiding out somewhere and now he's shown himself again."

"Burke!" she said reprovingly. "Don't try to shut your mind to the truth! There's a full moon tonight."

He eyed her uneasily. "Let's not get back to that kind of talk."

Her voice rose to a note close to hysteria. "Burke, that wasn't Tim Mooney! You should know that! It was Derek Collins! The Derek Collins we released from the grave!"

"You're upset and hysterical!"

"I'm both and I admit it," she told him. "But I also know what I saw here just now. The face even resembles the one in the portrait at Collinwood."

Burke glanced around as if to make sure no one had heard her and when he was satisfied that the center of attention was the bandstand, he said in a low urgent tone, "Don't repeat any of that to Sergeant Sturdy or anyone else. They'd call you insane."

She pleaded with him, "But oughtn't they be warned? I might have saved that wrestler's life if I'd told him."

Burke's handsome face showed disdain. "Do you imagine for a moment that he or anyone else would have listened to a wild story about a zombie?"

"I could have tried."

"It would have gotten you nowhere."

"But we are responsible," she said. "What's to be done?"

His arm around her tightened. "We can talk about that later. Right now I want you to pull yourself together. Everyone here is blaming what happened on Mooney. And you'll do well to go along with them."

"When I know better?"

"Yes," he said tensely. "We'll have to work this out later. On our own. Right now you'll be well advised to keep silent."

She gave him a warning look. "The sergeant suspects I'm holding information back. You know that."

"Let him suspect," Burke said bitterly. "This is more his problem than ours."

"How can you say that, knowing what we both know?" Their hurried exchange was brought to an end by the return of Sergeant Sturdy, who strode toward them from the darkness, an expression of perplexity and disappointment on his broad, tanned face. "I lost him," he said, glancing at the melee around the bandstand.

"Your bullet couldn't have hit him," Burke suggested. The sergeant looked grim. "It hit him all right. And in a vital spot. But it didn't do him any harm. Or didn't seem to. He loped off into those woods before I could get anywhere near him."

"Maybe he'll collapse later and you'll find him," Burke said. "I'm not counting on it," the sergeant said tersely and he left them to head for the bandstand, where order was badly needed.

Burke said, "Let's get away from here," and he guided her back toward the main fairgrounds.

A pall of gloom had come over the festive gathering. People milled about discussing the killing of the wrestler. The merry-go-round was halted and its music silenced. The other rides were equally still and there were no cries from the proprietors of the various games of chance. Everybody seemed numbed by the violence that had taken place and yet no one seemed ready to leave the fair.

Burke guided her along on the outskirts of the crowd. "We'll find my car and get away from here as quickly as we can," he said.

She stared at the oddly silent row of carnival tents and said, "No one will ever forget this June Fair."

"Not likely," he agreed.

"And of course they're all blaming it on Mooney," she said.

"Who else is there to blame?" he asked. They had reached the parking lot, which was dark and deserted in contrast to the nearby lighted area. There seemed to be no one near the long rows of shining cars. Apparently the ones in charge of the lot had rushed over to the main grounds on hearing about the murder there. Burke turned to her. "You wait here," he said. "I'll find my car and drive back for you."

"Don't be long!" she begged.

"It won't take more than a few minutes," he promised as he hurried off down one of the lanes between the densely parked autos.

She stood there nervously, her eyes trying to follow Burke, but he had temporarily vanished in the vast sea of cars. And then suddenly she heard the crackling sound of a bush being moved. She was so near the edge of panic that she almost screamed. Warily she turned in the direction from which the sound had come and saw only a clump of thick bushes.

But even before her pounding heart could quiet, the noise came again, louder this time, from the same spot. Eyes widened with horror, she stared fixedly at the dark bushes. A head and shoulders suddenly took form. She could clearly distinguish the flowing yellow hair and the round, strangely expressionless face. It was too much. She gave a wild scream and ran down the lane along which Burke had disappeared. She'd gone only a short distance when Burke drove up in the convertible and stopped to let her get in.

"I didn't expect you down here," he began. Then, seeing her state as she got in beside him, he asked, "What now?"

She was sobbing. With an effort she said, "I saw her!"

"Her?"

"Esther Collins!"

"You're allowing your nerves to run away with you," he reprimanded her sharply.

"It's true, I tell you," she protested. "Just where I was standing. She was hiding in the bushes."

He bent over the wheel, grim-faced. "That's as wild as your other story."

"It had to be her. I saw her yellow hair and her face has that same awful look about it. The face of a dead person!"

"If you saw anyone it was Nora Sonier."

"No!" she shook her head. "It was Esther looking for him. She'll have to wait until the crowd goes and then join him in the woods."

Burke had driven the car to the spot where she'd been waiting. Now he said, "I'll get out and take a look around."

"You won't find her," Victoria promised in advance.

"I don't expect to," he said. "But I'll look anyway." And he left the car.

She waited, sick with apprehension. She watched him as

he advanced to the bushes and probed among them. After a while he slowly walked back to the car. As he took his place behind the wheel again, she asked, "Well?"

"Nothing," he said and started the engine.

On the drive home they sat most of the time in the same numbed silence that had overtaken all the fair crowd. But as they headed down the private road to Collinwood she felt that some things must be said.

She asked him, "What are we going to do?"

"Wait and see if they catch the murderer."

"And if they don't?"

"We'll decide then what is best," Burke said from the wheel. "I want you to get over this shock and have a night's sleep before you make any decisions."

"I know what we should do," she said quietly. "Tell everything to Sergeant Sturdy."

Burke shook his head. "You don't know what you're saying or what it could lead to."

"I don't enjoy the position I'm in now."

"Have you wondered how much of this is truth and how much imagination? Of all the people who saw the murder tonight how many do you think will say it was Mooney who climbed onto the bandstand and snapped that man's back?"

"I don't know," she faltered.

"I'll tell you," he said. "They'll all think it was him with one exception. And that exception will be you. Do you expect the sergeant to take your word against all the others?"

"The others can't guess, because they don't know," she protested. "We know about the vault and what happened there. Surely you must believe it was Derek Collins in zombie form who appeared tonight?"

Burke brought the car to a halt, in front of Collinwood. "I'm sorry, I don't agree," he said. "It was Mooney, more dangerously mad than ever."

"You want to say that!"

"Until I have more evidence I have to say it," he told her. He studied her seriously. "I think you're allowing this zombie business to become an obsession with you."

"I'll give you a few days, Burke," she said carefully. "No more. If this violence goes on and nothing is done to stop it by then I'm going to see the sergeant and tell him my story. I don't care whether he believes it or not."

"Fair enough," Burke said quietly. "We'll see what tomorrow brings." He escorted her to the door and kissed her goodnight. Inside she found the others still up and gathered in the hallway in a spirited discussion of the happenings at the fairgrounds. Her entrance was a signal for them to go over it all again.

Elizabeth stared at her. "And you were right there by the bandstand when it happened?"

"Yes," she said.

David was all excited. "I wish I'd been there," he said. "I miss all the fun."

Roger Collins gave his son a reproachful glance. "Seeing a man murdered could hardly be classified as fun, young man."

The boy looked crestfallen. "You know what I mean," he mumbled.

Carolyn said, "I think we should all get to bed. I don't see what good we're doing hashing it over again and again."

"Sound idea," Roger agreed. To David, he added, "Especially for you, son."

They straggled upstairs with Elizabeth in the lead, saying, "I don't expect I'll sleep at all."

Roger and Victoria were in the rear. He halted to turn out the lights in the lower hallway, leaving only the night light on over the stairs. Then he joined her, saying, "I suppose you were with Burke Devlin."

"Yes, Burke and I went to the fair together," she said, wondering what he was getting at.

He smiled sarcastically. "Your heart has mended very well."

She paused on the stairs to stare at him. "What do you mean?"

He lifted an eyebrow. "We were all afraid you'd be crushed when Ernest was killed."

"I suppose I was."

"Yet it only happened a few months ago and you seem to have forgotten him altogether."

"That isn't true," she defended herself.

He shrugged. "Perhaps I've spoken out of turn. I often do. But Burke Devlin is such a different type from Ernest. Where Ernest was sensitive, Burke is strong and unyielding. I'm surprised you're so attracted to him."

"Burke has been a good friend to me."

"You have good friends here in this house," he said meaningfully.

She blushed as she realized he was speaking for himself. "I am well aware of the kindness *Elizabeth* and you all have shown me." She hurried on upstairs, leaving him to follow at a distance.

In her own room she considered what Roger Collins had said—but not in the light of any new interest in him. She was rather thinking of his comparison between Ernest and Burke. It had made her realize that she was dealing with an entirely different sort of person from the young violinist she had loved. Burke was stern and not likely to give in to anything. He had confessed himself interested in spiritualism and the world of ghosts but he would go no further than that. While she had become increasingly absorbed in the mystery of the unknown he was firmly remaining in an observer's role. She was ready to accept the existence of the zombies and he was denying the possibility. Perhaps it was good there existed a balance between them. But she believed if Ernest was alive he'd be much more sympathetic to her viewpoint.

Her dreams that night brought her visions of the giant with cold, vacant zombie eyes. Once again she was stalked by him and fled endlessly through a terrifying forest as he followed with his loping gait. At last she collapsed face forward on the rough ground with its covering of leaves and broken twigs. She lay there sobbing in fear as the monster reached her. Lifting her in his powerful hands, he brought her crashing down against his knee and snapped her back. She sat up in bed with a scream!

It was nearly dawn, with the first pink light of another day flowing into the room. She sat there wet with perspiration and trembling. Then, after a while, she forced herself to lie back on the pillow and tried to sleep again. After a short period of restless slumber it was time to get up.

Elizabeth, who was in the dining room when she went down, also showed the strain of the previous night. As Victoria helped herself from the buffet the older woman brought her up to date on the news.

"Both the radio and television gave most of their time to the murder," she said. "People are shocked."

"It was dreadful," Victoria agreed as she sat down with her juice and cereal.

Elizabeth shook her head. "They were all so certain that Mooney and that girl had left this part of the country. Now they know better."

"They do believe it was Mooney?"

"A few people said they didn't think it looked like him, but most of them claim it was Mooney," Elizabeth said. "After all, he's bound to look haggard and wild after being on the run so long."

"I suppose so."

"It has to be him," the dark woman went on. "Just before dawn this morning one of the state police caught a glimpse of him and the girl together in the woods. But they got away from him."

Victoria tried hard to hide any reaction to this news. But she could not help remembering the girl who had appeared in the bushes at the parking lot. And she was not surprised to hear that the two lost souls had finally found one another. Somewhere in the depths of the woods the zombies would be marking time in the shadows before venturing forth in the night again.

"It was all so senseless," Elizabeth said, breaking into her reverie. "Why would he do such a thing?"

"He must be mad," Victoria said.

Elizabeth sighed. "And the way he attacked you that night—he could have snapped your neck like a twig, I guess. You were lucky, it seems."

"I was, I suppose."

Elizabeth continued unhappily, "According to the story, Mooney deliberately broke his opponent's back. It was a malicious show of strength."

"I saw it happen," Victoria said. "It was exactly like that."

The older woman shuddered. "It makes my flesh crawl to think about it. And to know he's still at large."

"Yes," Victoria agreed soberly, "that is the frightening thing."

Elizabeth rose from the table. "We'll have to take all the same precautions again. I certainly hope he doesn't come back here."

"I hope not," said Victoria, who had been wondering about the same thing herself. It had worried her for reasons Elizabeth didn't know. The house and the cemetery had seemed an irresistible lure for the two living dead. Derek and Esther Collins kept returning to Collinwood.

On Monday Victoria had difficulty concentrating on her work. David kept turning from his lessons to pose questions about the murder and her thoughts concerning it.

But somehow she kept him at his tasks and it was finally late afternoon. She was free for a short time to turn to her own interests. But she was so confused that she hardly knew what to do.

She phoned Burke and reached him in his office in the village. "Is there any more news?" she asked.

"Nothing since this morning," he told her. "One of the police spotted them in the woods. But he lost them."

"I heard about that," she said. "I wasn't surprised. I mean, that she found him. They've always been together."

"Yes." His expressionless tone showed he didn't approve. "I'll come over tonight."

"I wish you would," she said. "I think it might be interesting to visit the cemetery and perhaps call on Amos Martin again."

"Expecting to find Mooney at either of those places?" he asked wryly.

"No. But maybe something more interesting."

"I doubt it," he said. "Anyway, I'll come by for you at eight."

When they were heading toward the village and had gone as far as the lane he slowed the car. "Are you really serious about visiting the cemetery?"

"Yes," she said. "I'd like to see if there are any changes at the tomb."

"There won't be."

"How can you be so sure?"

He headed the car along the uneven surface of the lane. "Because I don't think we released Derek and Esther from that vault. I don't believe they were ever in those coffins."

"It had to be Derek last night," Victoria insisted. "Who else would have committed such an insane crime?"

"Mooney."

"But some people had enough of their wits about them to recognize that the man who entered the bandstand didn't look like Mooney. That came out in the news this morning."

"People always argue about things like that."

"But what he did was so pointless. There was just no motivation at all. It had to be Derek. He was that kind of cruel person when he was alive."

Burke brought the car to a halt in the field. "You've got it all figured out your own way. What's the use of my arguing?"

"None," she told him.

They left the car and headed for the cemetery once more. It seemed as sad and isolated as always and she regretted that she had ever seen it. But Ernest was buried there and there was this other eerie business that kept bringing them back. Burke led the way to the vault and tried the door.

"It's latched just as I left it," he said, turning to her. "I told you not to expect any change."

But she wasn't paying any attention to him. She was staring at the ground leading to the vault. "Look!" She pointed to a series of footprints in the soft earth of the path.

He frowned and came back to her. He studied the spot she'd indicated. "Of course there are bound to be footprints there. Plenty of them. Ours!"

"Not those!" she said tensely, leaning down to indicate a special footprint.

Burke studied it. "Probably a distortion," he said. "It has rained since we've been here. More than once."

She looked up at him with a wondering expression. "You won't admit the truth when you're faced with it." She gave her attention to the footprint again. "That footprint is almost twice as large as any of yours. And there are more of them." She straightened up to follow them until they vanished on a harder gravel surface. Then she turned to him. "Derek has been back! Those footprints are proof!"

He was standing a few yards from her, looking forlorn. "If they're someone else's footprints, they're Mooney's. If my story is right, he did come here and break open the coffins."

"All right, Burke," she said sadly. "I guess I'll have to convince you some other way. Will you take me to Amos Martin's?"

"You're not going to convince me of anything," Burke warned her. "Why do you want to go to Martin's place tonight?"

"To see if he'll hold another séance for us."

"I've warned you that's fakery!"

"You say so," she told him. "That doesn't prove it." Burke was beside her now and he gave her a bitter smile.

"So you want to hear some words of wisdom from Mad Martin's Ma? Very well. Let's go!"

Victoria smiled at him with sudden warmth. "You only call him 'Mad Martin' when you're angry."

They found the old man in his kitchen, sitting there on his cot in the growing darkness. He seemed not at all surprised that they had returned and quite willing to cooperate when Victoria asked if he would try and summon the spirit of his mother again. Once again they all sat at the table with the flickering candle in the middle of it serving as the room's only light.

Martin's eagle face and towering bald dome seemed more eerie than ever in the glow from the candle. "I'm not always successful," he warned her. "There are times when we are not in tune. But I will try."

Burke's face across the table showed a look of grim amusement. She could tell he was hating the whole business. Amos closed his eyes and began to chant some weird ritual. She couldn't make out what he was saying, as he kept his voice very low. Then, as before, his head twisted to the side and he slumped in his chair.

In a moment that other voice, the high-pitched one he attributed to his mother, issued from the gaping black mouth. "I'm cold."

Victoria was trembling. She tried to hide her emotions as she asked, "Can you tell us about Derek and Esther Collins?"

The thin voice came again, "The woods are dark."

"What woods?" Victoria asked.

"I can see the Collins cemetery but I was buried in the village. In the village near the church."

"Are Derek and Esther in the Collins cemetery?"

"They are walking ahead of me. They do not know. They are

not able to see me. They are doomed to wander forever."

"Do you mean they are zombies?" she asked.

There was a long silence. She watched the thin, parchment face of the old man in the flickering light of the candle. But there was no sign of life. She glanced across at Burke, who merely shrugged.

Then the voice came clearly again. "Derek Collins hates the Blair family and all its sons and daughters."

"Why?" Victoria wanted to know.

"The Blairs reveled in his disgrace. Now he is free to avenge himself. But he and the girl are lost in the woods."

"Near the cemetery?" Victoria asked.

But there was no reply. And after a moment Amos Martin raised his head and blinked the rheumy, sunken eyes. He asked her, "Did I reach Ma? Did you get a message?"

"It was very garbled," she said. "I don't think I understood much of it."

"The spirits are not always able to make us understand," the old man told her.

Burke got up from the table. "Thanks, Amos," he said. "It was interesting." And he put another five-dollar bill down before the old man.

Amos nodded and took the bill in a trembling hand. He glanced up at Victoria. "Keep the crucifix by you," he advised.

When they were back in the car again Burke said, "Well, that didn't get you much information."

"She spoke about seeing Derek and Esther," Victoria pointed out. "She said they were doomed to eternal wandering."

"Amos told you what you wanted to hear," he said.

"And what about that mention of the Blair family?" she said.

He kept his eyes on the road. "Everyone in this area knows the Collins and Blair families have been at loggerheads for years. He just added that for a touch."

"I wonder," she said.

And she wondered even more the following morning when she met Elizabeth on the stairs. The older woman said, "Simon Blair died last night."

CHAPTER 9

Victoria gasped. The spirit voice had predicted that Derek Collins would seek revenge on all the Blair family—but no, this must be merely a coincidence. Elizabeth had seemed not especially surprised or shocked. There could have been no violence. Cautiously, she said, "It must have happened suddenly."

"He was an old man," Elizabeth said. "The broadcast said his death had been attributed to heart failure."

Victoria felt a surge of relief. So the death had nothing to do with the zombies after all. She said, "This may make it easier for you to buy his property."

The older woman smiled. "I'm sure it will. His lawyers were all in favor of the idea. And I can't see that it did him any good to turn me down the way he did."

"You mentioned that he had a strong feeling against any of the Collins family owning his land."

"He hated the Collins family," Elizabeth assured her. "He even brought up that old business of Derek. Imagine touching on a scandal a hundred years old as if any of us could be blamed for it."

"Some people are inclined to live in the past," Victoria said.

"Simon Blair was one of them. I don't think he ever enjoyed life. And he didn't want others to. I explained that an expansion of the packing plant would mean extra workers employed and more prosperity for Collinsport. He wouldn't listen. He really didn't care about the town."

Victoria asked, "Is there any word about Mooney?"

The older woman shook her head. "They haven't found him yet. They claim they've been combing the woods with a lot of extra state troopers. But I wonder just how hard they are trying."

"A man was murdered," Victoria said. "I think that would make them anxious to get him."

"Perhaps," Elizabeth said, sounding as if she was not convinced.

It was a sunny, warm day and the skies over the ocean were cloudless and blue. Victoria and David did some of the study work outside, which made it seem less like a task. When lunch time arrived, she decided she would take a walk to the high point of Widow's Hill. Carolyn asked if she might come with her.

The two girls took the narrow path skirting the cliff and Victoria paused occasionally to admire the scenery and fill her lungs with deep breaths of the fresh, tangy air.

"You don't get this kind of air in the cities," she told Carolyn.

"I suppose not," the younger girl said with a sigh. "But there are drawbacks about living in a place like this. We're so isolated at Collinwood."

Victoria smiled at her. "Many girls would give anything to live on this lovely old estate."

"I suppose you like it," Carolyn said, glancing at her as they strolled. "You don't have to stay here and yet you have."

"There is a good deal to be said for it," Victoria agreed.

"When Ernest died, Mother was terrified you'd go. And with David back again it would have been awkward to find him another governess."

"I'm fond of David," Victoria said. "I'm glad I stayed."

Carolyn smiled. "It has worked out well. You're seeing a lot of Burke Devlin."

"He's a good friend."

"I think you'll marry him," Carolyn predicted.

She blushed and protested, "There's nothing that serious about it."

"I'm sure he'd marry you in a minute," Carolyn said wistfully. "It will be years before Joe Haskell can afford to get married."

Victoria laughed. "Think of that as lucky. You shouldn't be in a hurry to get married. You've lots of time yet."

Carolyn pouted. "So Mother says! But I don't feel the same way."

"You'll be glad if you don't rush into marriage too soon," Victoria promised the younger girl. "There's college ahead for you and all kinds of male admirers."

Carolyn looked brighter. "Do you really think so?"

"I know it."

The other girl sighed. "In the meantime I'm not having much fun. I'm perfectly well enough to go back to school."

"Better to be sure you've had all the rest you need," Victoria told her. "You haven't been seeing any strange shadows lately?"

"The things I told you about I really saw," Carolyn said indignantly. "None of it was my imagination."

"I didn't mean to suggest that it was," Victoria said in a placating tone. They had reached the high point where the bench was set out on the jutting cliff, and now they sat down there for a moment's rest.

"What a glorious day," Carolyn said, staring out across the silver waves.

"Yes. It is very nice."

Carolyn pointed to the beach and Amos Martin's house. "You go down to see old 'Mad Martin' pretty often, don't you?"

"He's an interesting old man," Victoria said.

"I hear he believes in ghosts and all such things. And his mother was a spiritualist and held séances down there."

"That's probably true."

Carolyn gave her an appraising glance. "Do you believe in ghosts, Victoria?"

"A certain kind of ghost," she said cautiously.

"I do," the younger girl told her. "And I've seen them. I know it. Collinwood is a real haunted house."

"All old houses have that reputation."

"Collinwood deserves one," Carolyn insisted. "Did he ever mention our ghosts when you were down there?"

Victoria would have preferred to get away from the subject. She said, "You know what he's like. He rambles a lot."

"I don't know what he's like. Mother would never let me go down there."

"It is lonely along the beach road."

"Mother is so terribly careful of me I don't get much fun out of life," the other girl complained. "Now she refuses to let me date Joe again until that Mooney is caught."

"You should understand that," Victoria said. "You know what happened at the fair."

"Mooney is crazy. They should have caught him by now."

"He's very sly and dangerous."

"That's the second person he's killed," Carolyn said. "And they think that his girl, Nora Sonier, is still with him. I'll bet she gets a thrill out of it all."

"Not the kind of thrill I'd like," Victoria said wryly.

"Well, I mean it must be exciting and all."

"Running from the police with a vicious killer would be just a little more than that," Victoria said. "I don't think you should be jealous of the girl."

"I'm not really," Carolyn admitted, staring out at the ocean. "But it seems that nothing exciting is ever going to happen to me."

"You're too impatient."

Carolyn glanced at her. "It's all right for you. You've got all these interesting men in love with you. Burke Devlin is very rich and handsome. And even Uncle Roger is interested in you."

"You just think that," she said, not anxious to encourage any belief that she herself considered Roger Collins in a romantic light.

"He's not much older than Burke Devlin," Carolyn said. "And he has quite a lot of money."

"I'm sure he has," Victoria smiled. "But I'm not looking for a husband. I'm perfectly content to be a governess." She got up. "And it's time we were getting back."

The balance of the afternoon went by in a routine way. Victoria planned to rest during the evening because Burke Devlin was to be in Boston for the day and would not be returning until late at night. She was still on edge about the murder and the fact she believed Derek and Esther Collins might strike again.

She changed for dinner and found the death of Simon Blair dominated the conversation. There had been no further word of the circumstances, but Roger claimed the police had ordered an autopsy.

"They found him in his living room," Roger explained. "He stayed in the house alone and had a woman come in to do the work by the day and cook his meals. She left at six thirty every evening."

"When did they find his body?" Elizabeth asked.

"Not until she arrived this morning at seven thirty," Roger said. "He was sprawled out on the floor in the middle of the room."

"The radio said it was a heart attack," Carolyn informed her uncle.

"I heard that, too," Roger agreed. "But an autopsy is routine in these cases where someone is found dead alone. I imagine it was his heart all right."

"He didn't die from generosity or good will, that's certain," Elizabeth said in an annoyed tone. "He didn't know what those things meant."

Roger smiled at her from his end of the table. "You needn't worry about it. You'll have your new plant after all."

"No thanks to Simon Blair," she said.

After Victoria helped Elizabeth with the dinner dishes she sat in the living room for a short time reading a magazine. When she noticed it was getting dark she decided it was time to go up to her room. She was going to start upstairs when she saw a car coming down the road toward the house. The red revolving light on its roof told her it was a police car. A chill of fear went through her.

The car halted in front of the house and Sergeant Sturdy got out and came up the steps. She opened the door for him as soon as he touched the bell. He nodded to her in his quiet way and came in.

"Wonder if I might speak to Mrs. Stoddard and Mr. Collins?" he said. And he added, "I'd like to talk to you as well."

"I'll get them," she said. "Will you wait here?"

The sergeant and Roger Collins stood by the sideboard while she and Elizabeth sat opposite them on the couch. Roger had his usual glass in hand and was showing nervousness as he waited for the police officer to announce his business.

Sergeant Sturdy's deliberate glance took them all in. "You've probably heard that Simon Blair was found dead in his place this morning," he said.

"Yes," Elizabeth nodded.

The sergeant's brow furrowed. "It was given out in the news that he died of a heart attack. And I guess that is what did kill him—a heart attack brought on by fright."

"By fright!" Roger Collins echoed the words in surprise. Victoria felt the room begin to reel around her. Sick with apprehension, she tried to maintain a composed front.

The sergeant gave her a sharp glance. "The plain truth is that he was murdered!"

"Murdered," Elizabeth said. "I can't believe it."

"But it's true, just the same," the man in uniform assured her. "We found a rear door that had been forced open. Literally separated from its hinges. An autopsy disclosed that Blair's backbone had been snapped in two . . . exactly like that of the wrestler."

Roger's eyebrows raised. "You're saying that Mooney forced his way into Blair's place and attacked the old man, and Blair died of fright during the struggle."

"That's about it," Sergeant Sturdy said in a grim tone. "Whether he died before or after his back was broken doesn't matter much."

"But what was the motive?" Elizabeth asked. "Were there signs of robbery?"

"None at all," the sergeant said, his hands clasped behind his back. "In fact, that is what put us off at first. Nothing was upset. No damage done. No money taken and there was quite a quantity of cash in a strong box in Blair's desk."

"Another senseless killing to match the wrestler's," Roger Collins commented. "Mooney must be insane. I can't imagine why you fellows haven't rounded him up yet."

"It's not all that easy."

"But think of the danger people face while he is at large," Elizabeth said. "You'll remember he found his way into this house somehow and attacked Victoria. It was only good luck that I went up to her room and scared him off."

"I remember that very well, Mrs. Stoddard," the sergeant said in his sober way. "It's one of the reasons I asked that Miss Winters be included in this talk we're having."

Roger said, "There's always the chance he might try coming back here again. He seems completely crazed. And what about the girl?"

"No sign of her either," the sergeant admitted. "No doubt she's with him. They stay together most of the time." He glanced at Victoria. "You haven't recalled any other details that might help me, Miss Winters?"

She sighed deeply. "No. I'm afraid not."

"Too bad," he said, his eyes fixed on hers. "We need all the help we can get on this case."

Roger cleared his throat. "Concerning that, may I ask why you've come out here tonight? I assume there is a reason."

Sergeant Sturdy nodded. "There is." He paused. "When was the last time any of you saw Simon Blair?"

Elizabeth crimsoned. "I think I was the last one of the family to talk with him. We had a meeting at his lawyers' office in Ellsworth. He was present for the meeting."

"Yes, I've been told about that," the man in uniform said. "You and he had some words, didn't you?"

She shrugged. "We may have. I don't exactly remember. There was a dispute over my wanting to purchase his property. I was quite upset by his attitude."

"He didn't want to sell it to you?"

"No."

Victoria listened to the questioning and tried to think what the sergeant might have in mind. Apparently he was well aware of the feud between the two families and had wanted Elizabeth to confirm it.

Roger spoke sharply. "What has all this to do with Blair's murder?"

"I'm coming to that," Sergeant Sturdy said. He reached into an inner pocket and produced a small square silver box. He held it out so that it glistened under the glow of the overhead chandelier. "Any of you ever see that?"

Roger took it in his hands for examination. "I can't say I have. What is it?"

"A snuffbox," the sergeant said calmly and he took the

box from him and handed it to Elizabeth. "What about you, Mrs. Stoddard?"

"It's the first time I've ever laid eyes on it," Elizabeth said and passed the silver box to Victoria.

Victoria's hand trembled slightly as she accepted it. It had a pattern of leaves engraved on its cover and in the center of the pattern were the initials *D.C.* in Old English script. The initials had a terrifying impact on her. Through the fog of fear that had encircled her she heard the sergeant asking, "Does it mean anything to you, Miss Winters?"

She shook her head and handed it back to him without meeting his eyes. "No."

"So none of you know anything about it," he said, walking back to face Roger Collins.

"Why should we?"

"This snuffbox was found on the carpet near Blair's body," the Sergeant went on. "According to the woman who worked for him, Blair didn't use snuff and she had never seen the box before. And then there were the initials, *D.C.*" He paused. "For some reason I thought that last *C* might stand for Collins."

"Why connect us with the murder?" Elizabeth demanded.

He spread his hands. "I was only trying to do my job, ma'am. We attempt to fit pieces together. It's a little like assembling a jigsaw puzzle without knowing the design. And often we make errors."

"I can tell you that you have this time," Roger said angrily.

"If you'll give me a moment," the sergeant said in a quiet voice. "I was curious about this box and where it might have come from. So I took it to my friend in Ellsworth for appraisal, the same one who enlightened me on the earring I found. And I was astonished to hear that the snuff box was of the same period. At least a hundred years old. He could tell by the mark of the English maker."

Roger said, "This fellow Mooney probably dropped it. He's been carrying out wholesale robberies around here and probably has his pockets filled with loot."

"My very thought," the sergeant said suavely. "But those initials stuck in my mind. I couldn't get rid of the idea that C might stand for Collins. I was so childish about it I started looking up some of the old records at the courthouse. And to my surprise I came upon the name of a Collins who lived here just about a century ago and whose name fit the snuffbox. I mean Derek Collins, of course."

"I fail to see why any of this should interest us," Roger exclaimed with annoyance. "Nor can I understand why you waste your time telling us this involved story while the murderer is still at large."

"If you'll bear with me for just a few more minutes," Sergeant Sturdy said. "The more I thought about the coincidence of finding the antique earring at the scene of a robbery and the snuffbox at the place where a man was murdered apparently by the same criminal, the more certain I was that Mooney had somehow stumbled on a collection of family treasures. And I wondered if you had missed anything here since Mooney was in the house."

"Not that I know of," Elizabeth said. "Nothing was taken."

"I saw by the records that Derek Collins and his wife were buried in your private cemetery," the sergeant went on. "And I decided to take a look at their burial place. They have a vault, do they not?"

"Yes," Roger acknowledged. "It is the only large one in the cemetery."

Sergeant Sturdy nodded gravely. "I took the liberty of opening it and I have unpleasant news for you. The vault has been vandalized and the coffins stripped of any remains. Even the expensive oaken outer cases have been splintered and wrecked."

Victoria had guessed this might be what he was leading up to, but it was evident he still hadn't realized the meaning of what he'd found. Nor was he likely ever to delve deeply enough in the past to learn the dark legend connected with the deaths of Derek and Esther Collins—certainly not to reach the conclusion she'd come to that two of the living dead, the dreaded zombies of the voodoo witch doctor's magic, were responsible for the terror stalking the county.

Elizabeth's attractive face was shadowed with horror at the news. "What a dreadful thing for anyone to do!"

"Do you think Mooney and the girl were hiding out in the vault?" Roger asked.

"That's it," the sergeant agreed. "I think they spent a couple of nights there. I'd say he got the notion there might have been some jewelry buried with the bodies in those caskets and decided to rip them open. And that's how he came by the snuffbox and the gold earrings."

There was a silence in the room for a moment. Then Roger said, "What a macabre story."

"I agree," Sergeant Sturdy said. "I closed the vault securely again. But I felt you should know."

"We are deeply grateful to you, Sergeant," Elizabeth said with an air of apology now that she'd heard the facts. "And I can only hope you soon catch up with this madman."

Roger asked, "Why would he pick Blair as a victim? And why didn't he ransack the place and take his money?"

Sergeant Sturdy smiled thinly. "It is hard to read a madman's mind, Mr. Collins. But we have a couple of ideas on the subject. Either he thought he heard someone coming and was scared into leaving before he could ransack the house, or he is simply too demented now to behave rationally."

"That's more likely the story," Roger said.

"Now I must go," the sergeant told them. "I'm sorry to have taken so much of your time—and that I had to bring you such unpleasant news."

Roger shrugged. "Better that we know. I'll see you to the door."

"Thank you," the sergeant said. He gave Victoria a parting glance. "You're certain you have nothing else to tell me, Miss Winters?"

"No," she said in a near whisper.

He smiled. "Well, if you should think of anything you know where I am." He said goodnight to Elizabeth and her and then Roger accompanied him to the door.

Elizabeth gave a deep sigh as soon as she and Victoria were alone. "What an awful business! And what a strange man he is! Why did he speak to you as he did just before leaving?"

"He seems to think I may remember something more about what happened when I was attacked in my room," she said awkwardly.

Elizabeth frowned. "But you told him everything. You couldn't see much since the room was in darkness."

"I've explained that," Victoria said. "But he still keeps questioning me."

"He's an odd man," Elizabeth said. "But I'm sure he's competent and has a keen mind."

"I'm certain he has," Victoria agreed and as soon as Roger came back to the living room she excused herself and went upstairs.

As she opened the door of her room, she sensed the presence of an intruder. She waited in the doorway, wary of another attack, and then reached cautiously for the light switch. There was no one in the main room. She cautiously advanced to make sure there was no one lurking in either of the closets. There wasn't anyone!

And yet she had the feeling that someone had been there. It was too strong for her to shake off. She stood by the foot of her bed and scanned the room for a sign of something out of place or something missing, but again without any results. She was on the point of dismissing the odd sensation as merely the result of nerves made taut by the interview with Sergeant Sturdy.

She returned to the closet, this time to check her clothes. And it was then she found her trench coat and a matching rain hat were missing. She rummaged through the closet, thinking it might have fallen from its hanger to the floor, but there was no sign of the missing coat or the hat. She even tried the other closet, although she normally wouldn't leave the two items in there. They were surely missing.

Her first thought was that Carolyn might have borrowed the coat. The younger girl had gone up to bed early, so she wouldn't bother her about it until morning. It seemed the only possible solution to the mystery. But Carolyn rarely borrowed anything from her. And never without asking her permission first.

It worried her and she hesitated to change for bed. From the time Amos Martin had told her that the room she occupied had once belonged to Derek Collins she had been uncomfortable in it. She couldn't get it out of her head that the room might easily have some secret passage from another part of the house. The room she had first occupied on coming to Collinwood had had one. Maybe this room did, too. And the sinister giant who had attacked her had used that secret entrance to get in her room in the first place.

She decided to leave her bed lamp burning all night. After all that had happened she couldn't face the long hours of darkness in the room. As soon as morning came she would question Carolyn about the coat and hat. Things seemed to be coming to a crisis.

Gradually the zombie Derek was betraying himself. Twice he had left century-old valuables behind. The odd thing was that the police had no hint of what they were up against. They could not guess that the murderer they were trying to bring in was no ordinary mortal, but one of the living dead, as was the girl accompanying him.

She couldn't erase the memory of those weird faces with their vacant, staring eyes. Faces of the dead! And she and Burke Devlin were responsible for bringing them back from the grave. If that rusty iron door had not been left ajar for the moonlight to cross their coffins, the two zombies would still be imprisoned in the vault rather than creating panic in Collinsport.

What would happen if police in some other part of the country caught up with Tim Mooney and Nora Sonier? If they arrested the hippie and his girlfriend, would the police then be of an open mind to listen to her story? Surely if it was proved that Mooney and the girl were far away from Collinsport when the robberies and murders were committed, Sergeant Sturdy would agree that he was looking for two other people.

It really was her best hope—that Mooney and the girl should turn up in Boston or New York. Then she could go to the sergeant with some expectation he'd listen to her frankly fantastic story. And even if he did, what then? How did one go about bringing zombies to justice? She and Burke had brought them to the half-life of the living dead, but how could they be made to return to their graves again? No one had suggested a solution to that problem. She would have to talk to Amos Martin and pray he had an answer.

She did not sleep well but at least the night passed without anything more happening. As soon as she went downstairs she sought out Carolyn and spoke to her about the coat and hat.

The younger girl stared at her in surprise. "Why, no," she said. "I didn't borrow your coat."

"It's missing, then," Victoria said. "And I can't imagine where."

"Perhaps you left it somewhere?" Carolyn suggested helpfully.

"I don't think so. I'm sure I didn't," Victoria said. She tried to recall the last time she'd worn it and convinced herself she'd returned it to her closet.

To take her mind off the unhappy incident she forced herself to get an early start with David on his studies. She'd only been working with him for half an hour when Elizabeth appeared in the library doorway and told her there was a phone call waiting for her.

She took it in the hallway and was delighted to hear Burke Devlin on the other end of the line. "I'm glad you called," she said. "Things have been happening while you were in Boston."

"I know," he said. And before she could tell him about her coat, he went on, "Did you hear the latest news?"

There was a note in his voice that made her aware the news was grave. She said, "What now?"

"There's been another murder," he said.

"Oh, no!" She began to tremble again.

"Some teenagers were on the beach road last night," he said. "They'd been driving around in an old car belonging to one of the boys. They stopped for a girl hitchhiker and she got in the back seat with one of the boys who was there alone. The boy made a pass at her, according to the couple in the front seat, and suddenly they heard a groan. They stopped the car and the girl dashed out the back door and vanished in the woods. They found the boy on the floor of the back seat with a knife in his chest. He died before they could get him to a doctor."

Victoria swallowed hard. And in a small voice asked, "Who do they think it was this time?"

"They're blaming it on Mooney's girlfriend. The fellow and girl in the front seat only got a quick look at her but they mentioned the flowing yellow hair and said she had funny eyes." He paused and in a strange voice went on, "I thought this might interest you. The knife the boy was stabbed with was at least a hundred years old."

She closed her eyes and leaned weakly against the wall. "Esther!" she murmured.

"I doubt that," Burke said with a sigh. "Though I must confess I'm beginning to wonder about some of this myself. But the couple said the girl was wearing a modern trench coat and rain hat."

CHAPTER 10

Victoria closed her eyes and leaned weakly against the wall, the phone still in her hands. Burke's words had come as a shattering climax to the already terrifying news of another murder. For a moment she was able to make no reply as the full meaning of what he had said took hold of her.

At the other end of the line Burke questioned anxiously, "Victoria, what's the matter? Why don't you answer?"

She made an effort to think clearly and said, "Burke, I must see you."

"I'll come over tonight at the usual time," he promised.

"No," she said. "I don't want to wait that long."

"I'm expecting important phone calls," he told her. "I can't very well leave here for a while."

"Then I'll see if Elizabeth will let me use the station wagon and give me an hour off," she said tensely. "I must talk to you."

"Very well," he said in a puzzled tone. "If it's that serious."

"I must talk to you right away," she told him.

"I'll be at my office here in the hotel," Burke said. "Come anytime."

She put the phone down and then rubbed her hand across her forehead. She knew Elizabeth would wonder at her request for the car and time off but she was past the point of worrying. The situation was clearly too serious to hesitate. It was only too bad she couldn't frankly tell the older woman what was going on, but she hesitated to do that until she'd at least discussed it with Burke Devlin.

First she went to the study and gave David a reading assignment that would take him some time. Then she walked down the corridor to the kitchen where she found Elizabeth.

Facing the older woman uncertainly, she said, "May I have the station wagon for an hour? I want to go into Collinsport and take care of an important errand."

Elizabeth's attractive face showed surprise. She was standing by the stove mixing something in a small pan. She quickly removed it from the burner and gave Victoria her attention.

"Of course you can have the station wagon," she said. "Do you want to go now?"

She nodded. "Yes, if that's convenient,"

"It makes no difference to me," Elizabeth said. "Do you want David or Carolyn to go with you for company?"

"No. I've given David a study assignment and I'd rather not bother Carolyn."

Elizabeth studied her with mild concern. "There's no serious problem, I hope?"

"It's just something I'd like to take care of right away," Victoria said, feeling uneasy under the older woman's close scrutiny.

"Then go along," Elizabeth said. "Only do be careful and don't stop the car along the road for anyone. You've heard about the latest murder, I suppose."

"Yes."

"I heard the details on the radio before I started this pudding," Elizabeth said. "And Carolyn wonders why I won't let her go out with Joe at night until all this is settled."

"It is a bad time," Victoria admitted.

"None of us are safe until that Mooney and the girl are captured," Elizabeth said vehemently. "They must both be insane!"

"I won't be long," Victoria promised.

"Don't worry about that," the older woman told her, handing her a set of car keys. "You know the one that fits the ignition. It has the larger head. And take care!"

Victoria promised that she would. Quickly she left the kitchen and made her way out the back door to the parking area at the rear of the old mansion where the station wagon was kept.

Within a few minutes she had left Collinwood behind her and was on the way to the village. Sitting at the wheel of the big station wagon gave her some outlet for her frustration and she kept her foot hard on the gas pedal, driving faster than she ordinarily would have. All she could think of was reaching Burke and telling him about her missing trench coat and hat.

She had an idea he was no longer as opposed to her theory of the zombies as he'd been up to now. There had been a suggestion of this in his troubled tone when they'd talked on the phone. And she hoped that in this new mood he might find a way to cooperate with her in ridding the area of the terror which she believed they had unleashed.

As far as she was concerned it was time they owned up to Elizabeth and Roger what they had done. They should admit that due to their carelessness the vault door had been left ajar on that moonlight night, and that the shaft of moonlight had set Derek and Esther Collins free. The authorities ought to be told the same story.

Whether they chose to believe it or not was up to them. But Victoria wanted the full weight of her guilty secret removed from her conscience. She no longer felt able to bear it.

She drove down the main street of the village and parked directly in front of the hotel. Quickly she entered the old building and made her way up the carpeted stairs to Burke's suite on the second floor. She paused before the door and knocked on it gently before going in.

Burke's secretary, a young man with horn-rimmed glasses, rose to greet her. "Yes?" he said.

"Mr. Devlin is expecting me," she said. "I'm Victoria Winters."

The young man smiled. "Of course, Miss Winters. You may go right in." He opened the door to the inner office.

Burke was seated at his desk looking his usual handsome self in a smart gray suit. He wore his white collar well and his tie matched the color of his eyes. She at once felt shabby in her dark pleated skirt and black turtleneck sweater. She'd not given a thought to changing so anxious had she been to see him.

He rose from behind the desk and came around to greet her. She could tell by his expression that he was concerned. He eyed her worriedly. "You look as pale as a ghost!"

Victoria tried for a smile. "That's a pretty unhappy phrase, considering the circumstances," she said.

He gave her a kiss and then led her to an easy chair. "Sit down and relax," he advised her and then leaned against the side of his desk, his hands balanced on the edge of it as he fixed a serious gaze on her.

She looked up at him. "I couldn't wait until tonight to tell you what I found out."

"Go on," he said.

She took a deep breath. "That girl. The one who murdered the boy in the back of the car with a hundred year old knife was wearing a trench coat and rain hat, you said."

"Yes."

"When I went upstairs last night I discovered that my trench coat and matching hat had been stolen from my room."

He frowned. "You're certain?"

Victoria shook her head. "Burke, why try to make such a mystery of it? You know that I'm living in the room once occupied by Derek Collins. He came there once before and almost strangled me. It's logical that he came again last night, perhaps with the girl, and they took my things. I'm certain there must be a secret passage opening into my room. And if there is, Derek knows about it."

Burke raised a hand in a weary gesture of protest. "You talk about Derek as if he actually were alive."

Her eyes met his. "Don't you agree that he has returned to a kind of life?"

He looked away, staring at the view of the Collinsport wharves through his side window and the fishing boats docked there. He seemed still unwilling to face up to the true horror that faced them. At last he said, "I know there's something very strange going on."

"*That* is an admission!" she said sarcastically.

He glanced at her with troubled eyes. "Until this third murder I wanted to believe that it was Mooney and Nora. Now I'm not so sure. But to accept that Derek and Esther Collins have been responsible for these crimes is to go a long way."

"Things have gone a long way," she warned. "Or I wouldn't have left my work to come here."

He stared at her in silence a moment. "You honestly believe that we freed two vengeful spirits to bring about all this terror?"

"Yes. The night we had the last séance with Amos Martin the spirit voice mentioned Simon Blair. Within a few hours Simon Blair was dead!"

"I haven't forgotten that," he said quietly.

Victoria leaned forward in her chair, offering him a pleading look. "We can't keep this to ourselves any longer. We have got to tell Elizabeth and the police."

His handsome face was devoid of expression. "Do you think they'll believe us?"

"It doesn't matter!" she protested. "They have to be told."

"All right," he said with a sigh. "When?"

"As soon as possible. The Collins family should know first."

"I'll drive over tonight after dinner and we can tell them what happened and what may have been the result," Burke said. "But they'll think we're raving. They won't buy our zombies."

"We can try to make them believe," she said, rising. "Let them talk to Martin as well."

His smile was humorless. "Do you expect them to take 'Mad Martin' seriously?"

"I suppose not," she said, looking down.

"And after we've begun spreading this zombie story, I'm afraid we'll be placed in the same class with him," Burke warned her.

She looked up at him with a frown. "It's not as if they don't know there was a dark shadow on Derek's past. And a lot of mystery about the death of him and his wife. There was a mention of it in the family history that I read, and Elizabeth once referred to village gossip about their being zombies. The stage was prepared for this horror play a hundred years ago when all those things happened."

Burke shrugged unhappily. "I'll admit that more and more your theory seems convincing. But if it has taken me so long to come around to agreeing with you, how long do you think it will take them?"

"I don't know," she admitted.

He picked up an opened book from his desk. "I even bought some books on the subject yesterday. I haven't been able to get it out of my mind. Here is what W.B. Seabrook has to say about zombies: 'Once a zombie has been activated, the sorcerer must guard against its eating meat or salt. If a zombie tastes salt, it regains its faculties, remembers that it is dead and cannot be prevented from seeking its grave and dying again. They are used to work in the canefields like automatons, their eyes staring, their faces devoid of expression. The body, deprived of its soul, is of the walking dead, a corpse called up by sorcery from the grave, but empty of soul or mind.' So it seems that other quite sane people have come to terms with a belief in the walking dead!"

She was touched by the inner turmoil the problem had so obviously brought him. "You'll feel better about it once we've told the others. I'm sure I will as well."

"Don't say I didn't warn you," he said. "I'm certain it won't do any good."

But she drove back to the old mansion by the sea in a much relieved state of mind. Just the prospect of making a clean breast of things to Elizabeth was enough to make her feel better.

When she reached Collinwood she parked the station wagon in its usual place and got out to enter the house. But she was intercepted by young David who gave her a strange look.

He said, "I thought you came back earlier."

She smiled at the boy. "No. Just now. What about your lesson?"

"I finished it," he said. "I'm sure I saw you about ten minutes ago."

Victoria shook her head. "I was driving back then. Where did you think you'd seen me?"

His answer was prompt. "In the cemetery."

"In the cemetery?" She couldn't hide her shock.

"Yes," the boy went on solemnly. "I went for a walk after I finished my lesson. I decided to go as far as the back field."

"And?"

"I could see the cemetery. And I saw you there."

"You must have been mistaken," she told him. "It had to be someone else."

"I don't think so," he maintained stubbornly.

She hardly knew what to say. "You were a distance from the cemetery," she reminded him. "You couldn't possibly see my face plainly."

"I didn't," he admitted. "But I recognized your trench coat and hat and wondered why you were wearing them when it was such a warm day."

Victoria stared at him in silence a moment as a fresh chill of terror went through her. "It must have been someone else wearing a trench coat," she said. And then she asked, "Was she alone?"

"I think so," the boy said. "She was sort of walking slow and stopping every now and then as if she was looking for something."

Victoria swallowed hard. "Did you see this girl leave the cemetery?"

David shook his head. "No. She walked over the little hill in the middle of it and went out of sight. I waited for a while because I thought it was you. But she didn't come back."

She tried to appear disinterested and said, "Well, I wouldn't worry about it. Often strangers come to take a look at the cemetery."

"I don't think so," David said with a child's frankness. "And anyway, she was wearing your coat!"

"A coat like mine," she corrected him. Placing an arm around his shoulder, she walked him toward the rear door of Collinwood. "Tell me how you managed with your lesson," she said, to change the subject.

Elizabeth did not query her on her trip to Collinsport, although Victoria was certain the dark woman must have been curious about it. She returned the station wagon keys to her and then went directly to resume work on David's studies.

The boy's account had made her flesh creep. She was certain it was Esther he had seen—Esther in search of her husband. Her pent-up emotions made it difficult for her to get through the day.
In the late afternoon when she had finished with David, she found herself in the living room standing before Derek Collins' portrait. The mocking eyes and leering smile had come to haunt her. It was as if he knew he had been brought to a kind of life again ... as if he were reveling in the murder and destruction his zombie reincarnation was strewing after him.

The portrait was painted in the heavy dark shades of another era, which served to give the face a more sinister appearance, as if Derek Collins was watching her from the shadows. The heavy gold frame surrounding the portrait enhanced this effect.

She was standing there preoccupied with the weird, lonely

feeling the portrait always induced in her when she heard a light step directly behind her and turned to see Carolyn also staring at the portrait.

"What do you think of him?" the younger girl asked.

"He has the sort of face one doesn't soon forget," Victoria said.

Carolyn nodded agreement, her eyes still on the painting. "I agree. I understand he died very young. So that must have been painted shortly before his death."

Victoria said, "He was a captain, wasn't he?"

"Of the *Mary Dorn*," Carolyn told her. "She was one of the fastest ships in sail. For some reason the family sold her after his death and she was lost a year or two later in a bad storm off South America."

She recalled hearing these details from someone else. "Interesting," she said.

"I can't imagine why the family sold the *Mary Dorn*," Carolyn went on pensively, moving her eyes from the portrait to Victoria. "She must have been a lovely ship."

"It could be because Derek Collins and his wife died aboard her," she said. "People are often superstitious about such happenings."

"Especially so in this case. The *Mary Dorn* was at harbor in the West Indies when they died." Carolyn paused. "I've heard it was murder and suicide but I don't know who was responsible or why. Mother has never wanted to talk about it to me."

"It wouldn't be the most pleasant of subjects," Victoria suggested quietly.

"No," Carolyn agreed with a frown. "But one would like to know the family history, even the black parts of it. I must try Uncle Roger one day. If I get him in a good mood he might tell me something."

Victoria smiled. "I can understand your curiosity. But some things are better not discovered."

Carolyn's eyebrows raised. "Why do you say that?"

"I don't know."

"You must have had a reason!" Carolyn insisted.

Victoria glanced at the portrait again. "I suppose I said it because his face indicates a hard, cruel nature. You might be better off not knowing the worst about him."

"He may have been a rogue," Carolyn observed. "But I'd be willing to bet he was interesting. Probably the kind of person you'd enjoy meeting!"

Victoria had to bite her tongue to stop herself telling the younger girl she might consider herself lucky that she had escaped a confrontation with the evil Derek. But she said nothing. She was already beginning to feel uneasy about breaking the ground for Burke's visit in the evening and the special news they would be imparting.

She waited until just after dinner. Roger had come home early and begun a long round of martinis and so was in an ebullient mood. Joe Haskell was calling on Carolyn and she had been given permission to entertain him in the rear living room. As soon as Carolyn left the dining room to prepare for Joe's coming Victoria spoke to Elizabeth and Roger.

"Burke Devlin is coming over around eight thirty," she told them. "And he has something important to discuss with you both."

Roger looked astonished. "Not coming to ask for your hand, I hope?"

Victoria blushed. "Nothing like that."

"At least we've eliminated that worry," Roger said with a chuckle. "We can't get along here without you. You must know that!"

"Please, Roger!" his sister gave him a reproachful glance. And then turning her attention to Victoria, she said, "Just why is he coming to see us?"

She hesitated. "It's rather private. I think I should wait until he can tell you himself."

"I had planned to go back to the office," Roger said. "But if he's coming I'll wait for him."

"He'll be here, I know," Victoria assured the blond man. "He promised."

When eight thirty arrived and Burke had not shown up, she began to wonder if she'd been wrong to count on him. Elizabeth and Roger were waiting for him in the living room and she was beginning to feel embarrassed. Then the doorbell rang and it was Burke.

Dusk was at hand when she ushered him into the living room and Roger had already turned on the ornamental crystal chandelier that provided the imposing big room with light. He was standing by the sideboard with a drink in hand and insisted on mixing one for Burke before anything was said. Elizabeth had seated herself in a wing chair and Victoria decided she would prefer to stand, at least for a time. She signaled Burke with a glance not to put off their news too long.

But before Burke could say anything Roger spoke up with, "What do you make of this new murder? Worst violence the town has ever known!"

"It is frightening," Burke declared soberly.

"Sturdy and his crowd are to blame," Roger went on. "If they were doing their jobs properly they'd have caught Mooney and that girl long ago."

"If Mooney is to blame," was Burke's quiet reply. Roger's mouth dropped open. "You mean you think someone else may be guilty?"

"Yes," Burke Devlin said. "I think there is a strong possibility we've all been on the wrong track concerning this trouble." He paused a moment. "That is why I am here tonight."

"Go on, Burke," Elizabeth said. "Tell us."

Burke glanced at Victoria as if to seek support and then took a deep gulp of the drink Roger had mixed for him. After that he moved a few steps across to the portrait of Derek Collins. Indicating the painting with a nod of his head, he asked, "What would you say if I told you he was one of your murderers and his wife Esther the other?"

Both Elizabeth and Roger looked astounded. It was Roger who answered first. "I'd tell you you'd been drinking too much of the wrong stuff!

Burke smiled wanly. "I know how you must feel. But I'm going to have to tell you just that. It all began on a night a few weeks ago when Victoria and I were discussing Ernest's death and moved on to the subject of spiritualism. This led us to visiting Amos Martin and the holding of a séance. The next night we went to the vault where Derek and Esther were buried." He stopped and took some more of his drink, before he continued grimly, "It's possible that's where we made our big mistake and initiated this nightmare of horror."

In great detail Burke went on to tell them everything that had happened and what interpretation might be taken from it. He ended the account with the story of Victoria's coat and hat being stolen and later having appeared on the murderess. And he admitted that he had come to the point of believing in zombies.

There was a silence in the big room after Burke finished. Roger and Elizabeth exchanged glances and Victoria saw that they had both gone pale. Her heart pounded as she waited for some comment from them.

The first word was from Elizabeth. She said, "This is an extraordinary story you've told us, Burke."

"I realize that," he said quietly.

Roger turned to Victoria with an almost belligerent expression. "You back him up in it?"

"Yes," she said, with a slight tremor in her voice. "I was the first one to believe the zombies were responsible. And after Derek showed up at the fair and broke that wrestler's back I had no doubts."

Elizabeth stared ahead of her, seeming to be thinking aloud. "And Simon Blair," she said in an awed tone. "He was murdered in the same way. A broken back! And he had denounced Derek Collins as a slaver only a few days before."

"In the séance Amos Martin brought up Blair's name," Victoria said, standing at the older woman's side. "I wasn't surprised to hear what happened afterward."

Roger drained his glass and put it on the sideboard heavily. "We know that Derek was a scoundrel and he and his wife died under mysterious circumstances. But all this rubbish about special embalming and zombies rising from the grave is stretching things a bit far."

"If you accept part of the story," Burke said, "why not accept it all? There seems to be no other explanation for what has gone on."

"Mooney and his girlfriend are the explanation!" Roger said angrily. "That's plain enough without you two starting this demented story and bringing up all the soiled linen of the Collins past!"

"Roger!" Elizabeth reprimanded him. She turned to Burke and asked, "Just who else, besides you two, know about this?"

"No one," Burke said. "We decided to talk to you people first."

"I'm glad you did," Elizabeth said.

"Next we'll tell the police," Burke said.

Roger looked appalled. "Repeat that nonsense to Sergeant Sturdy and have him come here and third-degree us about a lot of things that happened a hundred years ago and can't possibly have any bearing on these crimes! It's utter nonsense!"

"I'm not as certain of that as you are," Elizabeth told her brother. Her attractive face showed the strain of the interview. "There are things none of us fully understands. And the circumstances attending the deaths of Derek and Esther Collins were shadowed enough to make anything seem possible. Victoria and Burke may not be as wrong as you think."

Roger was pouring himself another drink and didn't bother to turn to them. "I never thought I'd hear such gibberish!"

"There are some strange coincidences about all that has gone on," Elizabeth contended. "The finding of a hundred-year-old earring, a valuable gold one, at the scene of a robbery. The discovery of that antique silver snuffbox with the initials *D.C.* by Simon Blair's body and the fact that boy was stabbed with a knife at least a century old. It surely must mean something."

"I believe it means that the zombies of Derek and Esther are stalking Collinwood and the village," Victoria told her. "And we must find a way to stop them. That is why Sergeant Sturdy has to be told."

"I don't see that it can do any harm," Elizabeth said quietly. "Even if he should disagree, your information may help."

Burke Devlin gave his attention to Roger. "That leaves you the only dissenter," he said. "What do we have to do to convince you?"

Roger lowered his glass. "Make me believe in the existence of zombies?"

"Yes."

"Show them to me," Roger said. "I challenge you to do that."

Victoria spoke up. "Your son saw Esther this morning. He watched from the field as she moved about in the cemetery wearing my trench coat. He thought it was me."

Roger frowned. "It was likely some stranger who wandered by. And why do you say she was wearing your trench coat?"

"Because my coat and hat were stolen from my room on the night Esther was seen in that kind of outfit. The night she stabbed that boy!"

Roger Collins laughed unpleasantly. "You're asking me to believe that a zombie entered your room and stole your coat and hat. And then this girl, who has been dead a hundred years, wore your clothes to hail down the car with those teenagers."

"Yes," she said resolutely.

"It's too ridiculous to warrant discussion," the blond man said. "How would such a creature get to your room in the first place?"

"It was his room long ago," Victoria told him. "Amos Martin says the room I'm in now was once Derek's. And I'm sure there must be a hidden passage from the outside leading directly to it."

"Wrong again," Roger said loftily. "There are no such passages in this house. You've been listening to 'Mad Martin' too much, young lady."

"Roger!" Elizabeth rebuked him. "I can't allow you to lie in this fashion. There are a series of hidden stairways in Collinwood, as well you know!"

Her statement came as a shock to Victoria, who had known only of one. She could see that Burke Devlin was surprised as well. Roger angrily took a gulp from his nearly empty glass and glared at his sister.

At last he said, "Very well, I admit it. But what I said was also the truth. For all the entrances to those passages have been sealed off for years. They are never used now."

Burke Devlin stepped forward with a stern look on his handsome face. "To your knowledge was there an entrance to these hidden stairways in Victoria's room?"

Roger looked uncomfortable. "I believe there was."

"Could we take a look at it?"

Roger made no reply so his sister got up from her chair. "I'll be glad to take you up there, Burke," she said. "I think we should all work together to see that this dreadful business is settled."

She led the way and they all followed her upstairs. When they reached Victoria's room Roger took them to the larger of the two closets. Stepping inside he pointed to the far end of it and said, "That is where the door was. But it was sealed off when I was a boy."

Burke said, "Mind if I take a look?" Roger shrugged his indifference. Burke went inside and carefully examined the narrow end wall of the closet, which had almost been hidden by the rack of clothing. He put his weight against it and quite suddenly the wall swung back. There were exclamations of surprise from everyone.

CHAPTER 11

An odor of stale dampness issued from the dark opening. Burke Devlin turned to face Roger, "It doesn't seem to have been so well sealed, after all."

The blond man looked confused. "I don't understand it," he said.

Elizabeth spoke up, "Perhaps this entrance was overlooked when the others were closed off."

Roger shook his head. "I heard father discuss it and he was emphatic in saying all the passages and entrances had been sealed."

Burke came back into the bedroom. "Well, this one certainly wasn't. And I think it pretty well answers your doubts about how the zombies got into the house and up to this room without anyone downstairs seeing them."

"An unsealed door doesn't mean these monsters you speak of have to exist," Roger argued. "I still can't go along with your story."

Victoria turned to him. "But I was attacked by Derek Collins in here."

"By Mooney," Roger insisted. "If anyone used the stairs and passage to make an entry in here it was that murderer."

"Think whatever you like," Burke said quietly. "I'd like to take a look at this passageway. I wonder if there are flashlights available?"

"I have one in my dresser," Victoria volunteered.

"And there's one in my room," Elizabeth said. "I'll get it." She left them to do so.

At the same time Victoria went over to her dresser and rummaged until she found the small but powerful flashlight she always kept there. She returned to Burke's side with it in her hand.

Roger was still in a bad mood as he told them, "I think you should leave all this to the police. Your meddling and this preposterous story is just too much. You'll confuse the issue and do more harm than good."

Burke said, "I think we've kept silent long enough. Now the time has come to talk."

A few minutes later Elizabeth came back to the room with a large flashlight which she passed to Burke Devlin. She asked him, "What do you propose to do?"

"Explore the passageway," he said. "I want to find where it ends and the point where the intruders made their entrance."

"I'll be willing to bet you'll find it a dead end affair," Roger warned him. "You'll probably have to return up here to get out."

"That's what I want to determine," Burke said, and he turned to enter the closet again.

"I want to go with you," Victoria said, following him.

He gave her a troubled glance. "I'd rather you didn't. It may be rough going. At best it will be smelly and dirty—and it could be dangerous."

"That's one of the reasons I'm going," she said firmly. "I'm involved in this and I want to be part of it."

Elizabeth said, "Do be careful, Victoria."

"I'll be alright," she promised as she stepped into the closet after Burke and then trailed him through the secret passage door. Within the narrow stone passage the only light was from their flashlights. Burke was at least a couple of yards ahead of her and sometimes went out of sight as the passage made a sharp turning. She played her flashlight against the stone walls and the low curved ceiling which had more than its share of cobwebs. It was an eerie world of dark and damp.

When they came to the steps they were steep and narrow. From down ahead Burke called back to her, "Be careful. One of the steps is badly broken."

"I'll watch!" she promised, her voice echoing hollowly like his. Within a moment she came to the stair whose central part seemed to have been chipped away. It offered a danger to anyone coming on it unsuspectingly.

Once again the passage followed a level area for a while before another flight of stairs, as steep as the previous one, presented itself. She was gingerly making her way down them when suddenly there was a high-pitched squeak as something scurried past her feet and away. She gave a small scream and almost lost her footing. For a moment she sagged weakly against the damp stone wall.

Burke turned to focus the beam of his flashlight up at her and ask, "What's wrong?"

"Nothing now. A rat, I think," she said in a thin voice. "It's vanished somewhere."

"You'll likely run into more of them," Burke warned her. "I'll wait for you."

She made her way down the rest of the stairs and joined Burke. She said, "We must be near the ground level now."

"First floor, is my guess," he said. "I have an idea this goes all the way to the cellar before we'll find an exit. I've noticed a few doors along the passage but they were all sealed."

"How did the one in my room come to be open?" she wondered as she followed close behind him.

He kept playing the beam of his flashlight on the narrow passage ahead. "It may be that it was overlooked when they made the repairs," he said. "I noticed some flakes of broken plaster on the floor. It's possible the door was sealed and forced open lately."

She gave a tiny shiver. "It's cold in here."

"Bound to be," he said. And then he suddenly came to a halt, his head held tensely as he listened. "I thought I heard something," he told her in a low voice. "Probably just another rat, but let's take no chances. You wait here a moment and I'll go ahead and explore."

"I'd rather be with you," she said.

"No, wait," he cautioned her. "I'll call out when I'm sure it's safe."

Once again fear gripped her as she watched Burke move on in the darkness of the narrow passage. He turned a corner and was lost to her view. She waited and prayed that he was wrong, that there was no danger ahead. She tried to tell herself the sound he'd heard had been nothing more than the scurrying movement of another rat. But she knew this was unlikely. Burke must have noted something quite different to alarm him.

She kept her own flashlight beamed straight ahead as she waited with taut nerves for his command to join him. But there was no sound from the darkness into which he had vanished. Now she began to feel a growing panic. Suppose something had happened to him? Suppose the sound which he thought he had heard had turned out to be a real threat? The cruelly strong zombie hands might have reached out from the shadows to grip his throat and choke off any warning cry he would have made.

The silence of the dark passage was becoming unbearable

and despite the damp coldness, beads of perspiration formed at her temples. Each moment she was becoming more certain that Burke had met with some violence. She pointed the flashlight into the gloom ahead, trying to decide what she should do. Probably the wisest course would be to hurry back upstairs for Elizabeth and Roger. Neither of them had shown any interest in joining the exploration of the passage, but surely they would help now.

But if she left without Burke knowing, and he was all right, he'd be sure something had happened to her. It was a reason for waiting there and hoping that she might soon hear his voice— perhaps a cheery shout to tell her the danger had turned out to be imaginary. That would be the best possible outcome of this frightening moment.

What was keeping him so long? She couldn't think of any reason for the delay unless he had gotten into some trouble. It was becoming a question of whether she should advance or retreat. There seemed only a scant likelihood Burke was going to return.

Her nerves were so on edge that she found it hard to think properly as she deliberated what she should do next. Then it was suddenly settled for her by a heavy footstep almost directly behind her. Victoria wheeled with a loud scream and focused the flashlight on the spot from which the sound had come. And then she screamed again!

The beam of the powerful little light hit the vacant face of the giant male zombie only a few feet from her—the monster who had gone up on the bandstand that night to snap the wrestler's back like a dry twig. Now the great powerful hands reached out toward her and the staring eyes seemed not to even notice the nuisance of the flashlight. The sagging, drooling mouth and pasty, massive face completed the picture of horror. As the giant lunged forward at her she cried out again and turned and ran.

She called out Burke's name between sobs of fear, hearing the heavy footsteps coming close on her heels. Her attempt at speed in the cramped passage took its toll. As she rounded a sharp turn she banged against the wall and the flashlight clattered from her hand. She had no time to retrieve it but raced on in the utter darkness now.

She was almost ready to collapse weeping on the floor of the passage when at last Burke's voice came to her from just ahead. "Victoria! Is that you?"

"Yes!" she screamed. "Derek! Just behind me!" And with a final burst of energy she rushed on and managed another sharp turn.

It brought her in the beam of Burke's flashlight and in the next moment she was sobbing in his arms. Burke did what he could to comfort her as he kept the flashlight pointed in the direction from which she'd come. "It's all right," he told her. "There's no one following you now."

"I saw him!" she continued to sob. "The giant! He was in the passage back there."

He tightened his arm around her. "Let's get out of here," he said.

They went straight down the passage to another steep stairway which led them to the cellar. Burke expertly guided her along a corridor with earthen floor and wooden walls to a door and a flight of stone steps that led to the side cellar exit. Within minutes they were both standing in the cool night air, the nightmare of the passage behind them.

Victoria had recovered herself enough to ask, "What happened to you?"

He said, "I saw her. Esther!"

"Where?"

"Just ahead of me. My flashlight caught her running away. I followed her along the same route we used to get out here. She vanished somewhere in the bushes. I spent as much time as I dared trying to locate her and then I knew I had to go back to you."

"Then they were both in the passage," she said. "When he came after me he was on his way to join her."

"And we somehow got between them," Burke's tone was grim. "Well, we at least know where they are now."

"Do you think he's still in the passage? He must have stopped chasing me when he heard your voice."

"I doubt if he's there now. Collinwood is honeycombed with passages. Probably he's found another way out." Victoria shuddered as she stared ahead at the bushes in the darkness. "They've probably met somewhere out here."

"I'd expect that," he agreed.

"What will we do next?"

"Tell Elizabeth and Roger about our experience and then drive back to Ellsworth and see if we can locate Sergeant Sturdy."

They found Elizabeth and Roger back in the living room. Burke quickly told them what had happened in the secret passage. Victoria saw that they both were shocked. Whether they believed the two were zombies or merely Tim Mooney and his girl on the run, they realized the danger had come close to them.

Roger scowled. "You actually saw them just now?"

"Yes," Burke said.

"Where can they have gone to?"

"Not far away is my guess," Burke said.

"Then I'd better call the police," Elizabeth suggested. "We can't tell what they will do now."

"I doubt if it would do any good," Burke Devlin said.

"Victoria and I are going to see Sergeant Sturdy next. We'll give him a detailed account of what has gone on here."

Roger looked dubious. "He'll not swallow that zombie nonsense any more than I have."

"We'll see," Burke said. He turned to Elizabeth who was seated on the couch. "In the meantime, will you move Victoria's belongings to another room? I don't think she should stay in her present one since we know that door to the secret passage is definitely not sealed."

"I'll take care of that," Elizabeth agreed and she told Victoria, "You can have the room next to mine for the time being."

With this arranged Burke and she left and began the drive to nearby Ellsworth. The sky had been quite dark early in the night, but now the moon had appeared and was casting a silver magic over all the countryside. But this did not make Victoria feel any easier. The full moon was always the signal for the zombies to prowl and do their evil. Burke said, "I hope we catch Sturdy in his office."

"I hope so," she agreed.

The grim look on his handsome face showed in the reflection from the dash light. "It's exactly the kind of night for those two to cause more trouble."

"I've been thinking that," she agreed and gazed out the side window at the moon again.

It was five minutes to ten when they arrived at the jail in Ellsworth. Luckily, Sergeant Sturdy was in his office. He invited them to sit down with no show of surprise on his stolid, square face. Seating himself at his desk, he studied them in silence for a moment. Then he said, "So you've finally decided to talk."

Burke showed amazement. "How did you guess we had something to tell you?"

"I've known all along," the sergeant said. He indicated Victoria with a nod. "I could tell by her manner."

Victoria said hesitantly, "I'm not sure you'll be interested in what we have to say to you."

"The way this case is dragging out I'll listen to anything," was Sergeant Sturdy's resigned admission. "We've had all kinds of false leads and nothing we've been able to follow up." He leaned forward with his hands clasped on his desk. "Just before you arrived we got a tip Mooney and the girl are up near the Blind Lake district. I have a couple of men up there now seeing if there's anything to it."

Burke Devlin shook his head. "I think you'll find it's another blind alley," he said.

"Wouldn't surprise me," the sergeant said. "Maybe you can tell me where they really are hiding out."

"I can," Burke said. "They're at Collinwood. Only it's not

Mooney and the girl you're looking for. It's two people who lived a hundred years ago." And he began a recital of the events that had started with their entry into the vault, ending with their encountering the zombies less than an hour before in the secret passage.

When Burke finished there was a long silence in the office. Sergeant Sturdy said, "I've heard some pretty wild theories about this case. This line about cadavers stalking the night after being buried a hundred years beats them all."

Victoria reminded him, "I told you our story wouldn't suit you."

The police officer got up and glared at her. "Is this what you've been holding back from me all this time?"

"Yes," she said.

He shook his head. "And I thought you might know something helpful." He came around the desk to stand by them. "You've done exactly nothing to solve the problem," he said. "Worse than that, you've wasted my time."

Burke was on his feet. "You'd do well to send some men to Collinwood. Those two are hiding somewhere on the grounds. You might be able to round them up."

Sergeant Sturdy didn't try to hide his annoyance. "Something like rounding up the wind," he said. "I've never done very well against ghosts, Mr. Devlin. I'm just an ordinary policeman, not some ESP expert!"

"You're making a mistake in your attitude," Victoria said.

"Maybe I am," Sergeant Sturdy said angrily. "But to begin with, I don't believe there are such things as zombies."

"You saw the vault and the mess it was in," Burke reminded him.

"Vandals," the sergeant said.

"There was more than vandalism involved," Burke argued with him. "In addition to the coffins being splintered, there were no bodies in them."

"Probably were empty from the beginning."

"The records state clearly they were buried there," Victoria pointed out. "And how do you account for the coffins being ripped open?"

"Mooney was looking for jewelry and valuables. And judging by the earring and snuffbox that turned up, he may have located some pretty good stuff in those coffins."

"It wasn't Mooney who left those items behind; it was Derek Collins," Burke said.

"No good," Sergeant Sturdy said. "If you want me to go chasing phantoms you have to come up with some more convincing evidence."

"Simon Blair was murdered," Victoria said. "The Collins family and the Blairs have always feuded."

"You're saying Derek Collins did it because I found his snuffbox near the body," the sergeant said disgustedly. "I call that just dandy, with Collins being dead a hundred years."

She said, "Then you'll do nothing to help us?"

Sergeant Sturdy glanced from her to Burke and back again to her. "All right," he said. "I'm going up to Blind Lake to check on that other story. If nothing comes of it I'll take my men over to Collinwood when we come back. If we're really late I'll come by tomorrow morning."

"It won't do," Burke said with irritation. "They'll be off somewhere else by then."

"You think they might return to their vault?"

"I'd say that's hardly likely," Burke said quietly, ignoring the other's sarcasm. "And if something else horrible is added to the other crimes tonight, don't blame us!"

"I won't," Sturdy promised. "If I get through in time I'll bring my boys over to take another look at Collinwood."

Burke gave him a bitter glance. "You may be sorry about this before it's all over, Sergeant. Come along, Victoria."

They left the office and got into the big convertible for the drive back to Collinsport, both feeling depressed at the reception they'd been given. As Burke slid behind the wheel, he said, "I guess we'll have to face this alone."

"But what can we do?"

"I'm not sure," he said, starting the car. "But it seems to me the best person to look to for advice might be Amos Martin."

It was now after ten thirty. Burke kept his foot hard on the gas pedal and they lost no time getting back to Collinsport. When they swung into the side road leading to Collinwood the moon was as bright as ever. Neither she nor Burke said much.

Roger Collins had been as coldly skeptical as the police sergeant, but it had not been so important in his case. And Victoria was sure that Elizabeth was at least half willing to believe their account of the zombies returned to terrorize the district. If only Sergeant Sturdy had been a little more receptive they might have joined forces to bring this horror to an end. But they could look for no help from the authorities, it seemed. Sergeant Sturdy would continue attempting to capture Tim Mooney and the girl, Nora Sonier, even though those two might by now be hundreds or even thousands of miles away from Collinsport.

At least Victoria had the comfort of knowing that Burke Devlin was solidly on her side at last. There would be no more doubts on his part. They had both seen enough of the weird giant with his strange loping walk and the vacant eyed girl with the flowing yellow hair to know these were no ordinary criminals. They were not even ordinary human beings!

From the moment of shadowed terror in the captain's quarters of the *Mary Dorn* a hundred years ago when the voodoo witch doctor had bent over the bodies of Derek and Esther Collins, this horror had been in the making. The special embalming that had been given their bodies then, plus the spell of witchcraft that was part of the process, had kept them ready in their coffins for the moment when they would be freed to return as the living dead. The shaft of moonlight which Burke had unwittingly allowed to cross the oaken caskets had been the zombies' deliverance. The rest was the chain of terror and evil they had forged behind them since that fateful night.

They were driving through the woods just before coming to the open grounds of Collinwood. Burke glanced at her from the wheel. "Discouraged?"

"A little."

"So am I."

"They won't listen," she said. "And it's so stupid. If they'd open their minds and consider the facts they'd know we were right."

He smiled wearily. "It took me a long time to believe in your zombies."

"At least you weren't too stubborn to change your mind," Victoria said.

"I'm willing to admit I was wrong. But how to handle people like the sergeant is another matter."

"I agree," she said. "I thought we were going to see Amos Martin. We should have taken the beach road."

"I was so absorbed in my thoughts I turned in here automatically," he sighed. "I'll turn at the next crossroad."

Victoria leaned forward in the seat. "No. We don't have to do that. We can park the car at Collinwood and walk down the cliff path to the lower road. It's only a few minutes walk from there. On a moonlight night like this it will do us good. I wouldn't venture it alone but we'll be together."

"It would save going back over the same road," he said. "Then let's do it!"

When they reached Collinwood she saw that lights were still on in the living room as well as in some of the upstairs windows. She turned to Burke as he brought the car to a halt by the cliff path.

"They're waiting up for me," she said. "Should I go in before we visit Amos?"

"I think not," he said. "We don't want to be too late. He may be in bed as it is. And we may have more news for them after we see him."

"That's true," she admitted.

They left the car and Burke kept a guiding hand on her elbow as they made their way down the very steep and winding cliff path. The bright night made it less hazardous than it would have been otherwise. The moon was reflected on the ocean and there was an air of peacefulness about everything that belied their own desperate mission. It took only a few minutes until they stumbled down the last of the difficult terrain to the level of the beach road.

Now she and Burke strolled along briskly. The outline of Amos Martin's two-story frame house could be seen faintly ahead and to the left. The sound of their footsteps on the gravel road and the pounding of the waves on the beach to their right were the only noises to break the late night quiet.

Victoria glanced up at Burke. "Do you think Amos Martin will have any plan to help us?"

"I'm counting on it," Burke said grimly. "If there is a way to conjure up ghosts there must also be a way to destroy them."

"A weapon that will even combat black magic."

"Right," he said. "It seems I remember he said something about fire when we were there last time. Do you recall it?"

She frowned. "I think he did say they could be destroyed by flame."

"That should have been done in the vault before they ever got free," Burke said with a sigh. "We'll have to find some other way."

"Maybe Sergeant Sturdy will think it over and change his mind," she suggested hopefully.

What Burke might have replied to this she was never to know. At that moment the two dread figures suddenly emerged from the bushes beside the road. Victoria gave a cry of alarm and pressed close to Burke. Derek Collins, huge in the moonlight, and Esther, hardly less menacing, came slowly toward them.

The blank, expressionless faces and the staring eyes of the two betrayed them as not of the normal world. Victoria had never realized the size of the hulking monster with the long black hair until this moment. He towered over the tall Burke Devlin, his great hands raised to attack them.

Burke shoved her forward as he planted himself between her and zombies. "Run for the house!" he shouted. "Let Amos Martin know what's happened!"

She hesitated. "What about you?"

"I'll manage. Go on!"

She took a final look and saw that the giant was frighteningly close to Burke, who was standing his ground to give her a start. She knew he must have some plan in mind, so she turned and began running toward the old house.

The road was uneven and she knew it would be disastrously easy for her to stumble and fall or turn an ankle. Her heart was pounding from fear and exertion as she raced along. She hazarded a fall by looking back to see if Burke was all right.

To her terror she saw that the girl with the flowing yellow hair was following her and only a short distance behind. Burke's strategy of holding the two back had failed. Now it was going to be a test to see if she could manage the safety of the house before this creature of horror caught up with her.

Gasping, her side searing with pain, she stumbled up to the house and around to the rear door. She could hear the running footsteps of Esther close after her. She threw open the wooden door and ran into the dark kitchen.

"Amos! It's Victoria Winters! I need help!"

She heard the scratching on the door as Esther fumbled to let herself inside. In another moment she would be facing this creature of the living dead in the darkness. She shouted to Amos again.

This time there was a quavering reply from upstairs. "Up here!"

She stumbled over to the rickety stairs and started up them just as the door was thrown open and the staring eyes of the yellow-haired zombie searched the darkness. Then the thing rushed over to the stairs and started up after her.

CHAPTER 12

The creature mounting the rickety stairs on Victoria's heels uttered threatening guttural noises that struck fresh terror in her. She could almost feel the outstretched hands of the zombie clutching at her. Reaching the head of the stairs, she saw frail old Amos Martin standing by his bed in a room to the left. An oil lamp on the table provided a dim light through its smoky shade.

"Amos! The zombies!" Victoria cried out as she ran toward him.

The old man's sunken eyes showed a gleam of fear. He took a step forward and gripped the lamp by its base and raised it in his hand. Just then the weird figure of the girl with the flowing yellow hair appeared in the doorway of the room and began approaching them in an odd, weaving manner. Her eyes seemed not to see them; yet she came directly to where they stood, a cruel look on her clay colored youthful face.

Amos waved a thin hand towards Victoria and in his raspy voice said, "Over there by the door!"

Victoria followed his instructions and eased her way along the wall and back toward the door she'd so recently entered, the old man backing with her and still holding the lamp aloft as a kind of weapon. The diabolical creature with the yellow hair kept following them so that finally she was over by the bed and they had backed to the door.

Then Amos in a low aside said, "Downstairs!" And as Victoria hesitated, he repeated again, "Downstairs!"

"What about you?" she asked fearfully as the thing by the bed began to come toward them.

"Never mind!" The old man rasped and then as the zombie woman came dangerously close he poised the lamp and threw it to the floor just in front of her.

There was a crash, a breaking of glass, the splashing of oil and lolling tongues of flame shot up from the floor. The thing that had once been Esther Collins drew back with a loud piercing cry ... a scream of agony and terror. By this time Victoria and Amos were on their way down the ancient stairs. The screams kept coming from the bedroom above as they groped their way through the blackness of the kitchen to the outside.

"Where is Burke?" Amos asked as he tottered along with her.

"He was trying to hold off the other one, Derek, when I last saw him," she said.

They rounded the corner of the house to witness a sight that brought new horror. Almost directly in front of them Burke was struggling for his life in the grip of the crazed zombie. The giant Derek had Burke on his knees and the huge hands were gradually tightening on Burke's windpipe.

Amos Martin touched her arm. "The ax!" he rasped. "Get the ax!" And he pointed to the woodpile.

Running back to the woodpile, she found the heavy ax where it rested against a broad stump. But Burke had partly freed himself and the struggle between the two was so confused she was terrified to wield the ax against the zombie in case she might accidentally hit Burke. So she stood tensely on the sidelines, ready to strike a blow against the monster when she could.

During this time she had forgotten the house. But it was impossible to ignore what was happening to the shabby old frame structure. Flames were eating their way through the roof and all the second story was a burning mass. Then there were a series of unearthly screams and for a moment the agonized face of the woman with the flowing yellow hair was framed in an upper window.

She remained in view only briefly and then vanished. But she had been there long enough to attract Derek's attention. The towering monster gave a low moan of pain as he let go of Burke and raised his vacant eyes to the burning building. He stood there for a full minute as if transfixed and then with a great bellow of rage he plunged forward toward the house.

Victoria stared in terrified wonder as the giant hurled himself against the front door and crashed through it to disappear into the burning house. From the flame-ridden structure there came what sounded like a tormented beast's howls of pain. Victoria dropped the ax which she'd continued to hold and rushed over to Burke.

He was dragging himself up from the ground, his clothing torn, his face cut and bleeding. "Did he go inside?" he asked breathlessly.

"Just now," she nodded.

"The fire saved my life," Burke said, watching the rising flames.

Now the great yellow and red tongues enveloped the frame structure from top to bottom. Old Amos Martin stood watching the great fire, his eagle-like face grim as the flickering light played on it and he watched his home leveled by flames. Victoria felt a quick feeling of sympathy and concern. He had deliberately started the blaze to save her. Suddenly there was a crackling sound and the whole structure caved in and lost shape.

In the collapse of the flaming building she was sure that she briefly saw the giant figure of the zombie that had been Derek Collins in life. Above the crackling and hissing of the burning structure there came a final weird howl and then the fire itself seemed to ebb. The peak of destruction was over; they would soon be confronted by the dying embers of the building and huge clouds of smoke.

She turned to Burke with panic still showing on her lovely face. "They were both in there!" she said in a low voice.

"I know," Burke agreed, his eyes on the blazing building still. "I wonder what Amos will have to say about all this." Burke adjusted his tie and collar as he walked over to Amos Martin with Victoria following. The old man turned to them as they came near him. His thin parchment face showed an expression of resignation.

"It is all over now," he told them.

Burke said, "I'm sorry about your house."

"Yes," Victoria chimed in, "he threw the lamp at Esther to save me. She followed me right up to his room."

The frail old man's eyes shifted to the flames again. "There could be no other ending," he said solemnly in his rasping voice. "They had to be consumed in the fire."

Burke was studying the remains of the burning building with the old man. "They were both in there when it collapsed," he said. "They couldn't possibly have gotten out."

Victoria asked, "Are we free of them at last?"

"For all time," Amos Martin said turning to her with a gleam in his sunken old eyes. "They are no longer sentenced to roam as the living dead. Now they will know their first blessed peace in a hundred years."

Burke gave the old man a meaningful glance. "So that ends the minder and the terror. I'm sorry it cost you such a price."

"I'm an old man," Amos Martin said. "Soon I will not need a home any more. In the meantime I will find a bed somewhere."

"I'm certain of that," Victoria said. "I'm sure Elizabeth will fix a room for you at Collinwood. Matt Morgan is the only one in the servant's quarters and there are a lot of vacant rooms."

"You needn't worry, Amos," Burke agreed. "We'll work this out so you'll not suffer."

Victoria saw that the flames had died down a great deal in the previous few minutes. She asked Burke, "What do we do now?"

Burke frowned. "We've got to get Amos up to Collinwood. And he'll never manage the cliff path. I'll go back up for the car while you stay here with him."

So Victoria found herself alone with the old man while they waited for Burke Devlin to get the car and return. They made themselves a temporary bench of a sawhorse. Sitting side by side on it, they watched the blaze.

Victoria's voice was hushed as she gazed into the fire. "Do you think we'll find any trace of them?"

"Not in that inferno," Amos Martin said. "It's better this way."

"I'm glad they're at rest."

He nodded. "I knew it would happen just as it did."

She stared at him in surprise. "You knew?"

"Yes. My Ma came to me last night and told me they would die in flames. And the flames would be of my making."

Victoria felt a chill of the unknown as she listened to him talk so easily about this message from the spirit world—a message which had turned out to be only too true. She guessed that Burke might accuse the old man of indulging in hindsight to make it seem he had strong spiritual powers. But she was ready to believe his story. She said, "They must have seen the flames from Collinwood."

"And from the village as well," the old man said. "Mine was the last of the shore houses. They're all gone now."

"You mustn't worry," Victoria said. "We'll see you get a comfortable place. You'll be better off living where you can get some care."

His eagle face showed no expression. "It makes no difference to me," he rasped. "I have those in the other world that stay by me. I will get my messages wherever I may be."

Sitting there beside the old man in the flickering light of the dying blaze, she could not help but be impressed by his courage. His clear thinking had saved her life and that of Burke's. They would always be deeply indebted to him.

The whole weird business had started in the old frame house. It had been here that she'd first heard of Derek and Esther Collins and that tragic night when murder and suicide began it all in Barbados. The drama had moved far from that time when the *Mary Dorn* had been resting at the dock of the West Indian island. And she and Burke had been caught up in it.

Three murders had taken place since the zombies had been freed to stalk the village and Collinwood. Now it would end. The story of these terrible days and nights would be repeated until they became a legend as powerful as the original. But how to explain all this to the authorities? Especially in view of the dour reaction Sergeant Sturdy had given them earlier in the evening.

She saw Burke's headlights as he came down the beach road toward them. Standing, she asked the old man, "Is there anything you want to take with you?"

He shook his head. "Everything that I valued has been lost in the fire. I'll go just as I am."

She walked with him to the car. Burke helped Amos into the back seat and then held the door open for her to get in the front seat beside him. He slipped behind the wheel and headed the car back toward Collinwood.

"I wonder what Elizabeth and Roger will have to say?" he asked.

"I doubt they'll believe our story," she said.

He smiled wryly. "It wouldn't be the first time. Anyway, I feel a lot better. It's like a weight being lifted from me."

"I know," she said.

"I'm cured of visiting vaults," he said. "Never again!"

"About time."

As they drove along, Burke called back to Amos in the rear seat, "We've tried to explain about the zombies to the people at Collinwood and the police but they wouldn't listen."

"I can understand their being skeptical."

"Now they must give us a hearing."

"I wouldn't count on it," Amos Martin told him. "They will try to seek their own explanation."

"But the fire and the zombies perishing in it make it a matter of record now," Burke protested.

Victoria gave him an anxious look. "You're forgetting something."

"What?"

"We three are the only ones who saw Derek and Esther Collins consumed by the flames. Aside from us there were no witnesses."

From the rear old Amos said, "The girl speaks the truth."

Burke frowned at the wheel. "But if the murders and plundering ends they'll have to accept our version of things."

"I don't think so," Victoria said.

"What will they say?" Burke asked with some impatience.

"They will simply reply Mooney has gone into hiding for a time again," she said. "They've made up their minds Mooney is guilty and they'll not be quick to change."

"Mooney and the girl," Amos said in his raspy voice. "Aye! There'll be those who will still insist they be given the blame."

"But that's ridiculous!" Burke protested. "We know better."

"Aye! We do," Amos Martin acknowledged.

"That's a long way from convincing others," Victoria said quietly.

"Elizabeth will have seen the fire," Burke said. "She'll know that something has gone wrong."

When they reached Collinwood Elizabeth welcomed them at the front door. "We've been watching the fire from the upper windows. How awful for you, Amos."

"I'm afraid he lost everything," Victoria said. "I knew you would be able to find a place for him here."

"As long as you like, Amos," the older woman said solicitously, guiding the old man to an easy chair in the living room. "You have always had your home on Collins land and you shall certainly not be homeless now."

The old man settled himself in the chair, looking strangely out of place in the rich surroundings and seeming more frail than ever. The eagle face took on a sad smile. "I have lived all my life within sight of Widows' Hill."

"Indeed you have," Elizabeth agreed. "I remember going down there as a little girl. Your mother was alive in those days."

"Aye," the old man nodded. "Ma lived to a ripe age."

Burke who had been standing in the background smiled. "Amos is of a ripe age himself," he said. "And to be honest and fair to him, he lost his house while saving our lives."

Elizabeth gave him a close scrutiny. "My! What happened to you! You look as if you'd been in a fight. Did that come from battling the fire?"

Victoria shook her head. "That damage was done before the fire."

Before she could enlarge on this Roger came into the room, followed by Carolyn. Both showed curiosity in what had happened and Roger insisted that all the men should have a good stiff drink.

"Just the thing for a shock like you've had," he said as he passed a strong glass of rum to Amos.

Burke took a sip from his own glass and regarded the group.

"I think it's time you heard some of the details."

Roger looked mildly annoyed. "Don't tell me this wasn't just a simple case of fire with no bizarre complications!"

Elizabeth had seated herself with Carolyn on the couch. Now she gave Burke a weary smile and said, "Roger is right, you know. I think it would be too much if there were any ghosts associated with the fire. We've had enough of them and hidden passages as well." She turned to Victoria who was standing behind Amos Martin's chair. "By the way, Victoria, I've shifted your things to the room next to mine as I promised."

"Thank you," Victoria said quietly, anxious to have Burke get on with what he was trying to say.

Roger spoke over his glass. "Well, let's hear the rest of it."

"There will be no more murders," Burke said quietly. "And no more robberies or terrorizing of the countryside."

Roger's eyebrows raised. "And what has brought about this happy turn of events?"

Burke paused and then said, "I know you're not going to believe this. But the zombies perished in that fire just now."

"Whatever are you saying?" Elizabeth demanded. "Derek and Esther Collins were in that burning house when it collapsed." Burke turned to Victoria and Amos Martin. "These two will corroborate."

Elizabeth looked at her with worried eyes. "Well, Victoria?"

"He's right," Victoria said. "The zombies were waiting for us on the beach road. They chased us to the house. In protecting me, Amos was forced to throw a lamp at Esther Collins. It crashed on the floor and started the fire. The flames and Esther's being trapped in them drew Derek into the house. They never came out."

Roger remarked lightly, "Now I call that neat. First you dream up these zombies and then you find a means of disposing of them. Very smart, indeed."

Amos Martin spoke up in his rasping voice. "They are telling you facts, Mr. Collins. I can vouch for them."

"We all know your reputation for seeing spirits, Amos," Roger said dryly.

Elizabeth looked at Burke reproachfully. "It really is a tall story, Burke. Don't you think it would be best forgotten?"

Carolyn looked around with the indignation of the young. "I think it's awful calling Burke and Victoria and Mr. Martin liars. I'm sure they're telling the truth. I know something dreadful has been going on here. I saw some kind of ghost one night on the lawn."

Roger made a weary gesture with his free hand. "You see how all this nonsense builds? Let the impressionable hear any of this and we'll have a first class scandal going!"

Carolyn jumped up. "And I'm not impressionable!" She

moved across to Derek Collins portrait and stared up at the leering face with its wild, mocking eyes. "I always knew he was bad. None of you would ever tell me anything about him."

"That will do, Carolyn," Elizabeth reprimanded her.

Her pretty daughter turned to regard her angrily but said nothing.

It was Roger who picked up the argument. "You say a man and a woman attacked you tonight on the beach road and afterward perished in the flames?"

"Yes," Burke said.

"In which case I say the two were not what you so colorfully dub zombies, but the escaped criminal Tim Mooney and his girl." Roger looked pleased with himself. "That settles your story. And it seems to me you should let the authorities know what's happened."

Elizabeth nodded. "Roger is quite likely right this time," she said. "Anyway, we can be thankful that one way or another all this is at an end."

Old Amos spoke from his chair. "There will be no more killing."

Roger nodded. "That is good enough news for one night."

Burke shrugged. "If this is the way you want it, I suppose it will have to do. But Victoria and I have been involved in this from the beginning. We have a clear picture in our minds of all that happened."

From outside there was the sound of a car pulling up in the driveway. And Victoria suddenly recalled that Sergeant Sturdy had promised to come by the house if it wasn't too late after he'd finished his investigation in the Blind Lake district.

Elizabeth stood up. "Who could that be?"

"Probably someone from the village wanting to know about the fire," Roger suggested calmly.

Victoria spoke up, "I think it's Sergeant Sturdy. When Burke and I called on him tonight he said he'd come over later if he could." Elizabeth looked dismayed. "But we don't need him now."

The doorbell rang and Roger in an exasperated tone told Victoria, "You'd better let him in."

As soon as Victoria opened the door she could tell that the sergeant was in a good mood. His broad, weathered face wore a thin smile as he stepped inside. "I guess I'm not too late," he said.

"No," she told him. "We're all up. We had a fire near here. Amos Martin's house burned down."

"I heard there was a fire on the beach road," the sergeant said. "And I guessed it might be the Martin place."

Victoria led him into the living room and he seemed pleased to find them all together. He greeted everyone and offered Amos his sympathy regarding the loss of his home. Then he glanced around at them all with an air of triumph.

"I don't usually make calls as late as this unless there's an emergency," he said. "But I thought I should get over here and tell you folks the news as quick as I could." He paused dramatically. "You don't have to worry about murderers being on the loose any longer."

Elizabeth looked startled. "How did you hear about it, Sergeant?"

It was the police officer's turn to show surprise. "I heard about it, madam, because I was on the scene when the end came for those two."

"Marvelous!" Roger said with a withering glance for Victoria and Burke. "Go on. Tell us all about it, Sergeant."

"Well," the stocky man said, "I told Mr. Devlin and Miss Winters that I had a tip Mooney and the girl had been seen heading toward Blind Lake."

"I remember," Burke agreed.

"Mooney was driving a stolen car. My men took up the chase and it lasted for about ten minutes. Mooney was driving on the road that skirts Blind Lake. He had her hitting over a hundred when he struck a curve and lost control. The car with him and the girl in it plunged over into the lake."

Roger said, "How long ago did this happen?"

"Maybe about an hour and a half back," Sergeant Sturdy said. "Well, I don't have to tell you people that Blind Lake has no bottom at all. It's just a mess of quicksand there."

"Always has been," Elizabeth agreed.

"Yes, ma'am," the sergeant said. "So the chances of our ever bringing out the car or those bodies are nil. But we know what happened and we won't have to worry about innocent folks being killed and robbed."

"In other words, Mooney and his girl have simply vanished from the face of the earth," Roger said.

"That's right, Mr. Collins," the sergeant said. And glancing across to Burke and Victoria, he added, "So that should take care of a lot of fancy theories some people have been getting about who committed all those crimes."

"I thoroughly agree," said Roger, who was clearly delighted by the officer's biting words. "And I'm glad it's settled."

"I wanted you folks to be the first to know," the sergeant went on. "I mean because Mooney vandalized that vault in your cemetery, which was a pretty awful thing to do. And he stole those pieces of jewelry from the caskets, which is about as low as a man can get."

Burke Devlin said suddenly, "And the bodies, Sergeant. You will remember they were missing as well. Do you think that Mooney stole the bodies along with the jewelry?"

The sergeant frowned. "I haven't figured that one out."

"I have," Roger said in his mocking way. "A hundred years! Naturally the bodies had completely disintegrated. It's what one would expect."

Sergeant Sturdy looked relieved. He glanced at Burke again. "Well, I guess that settles that," he said. "No mystery there."

"No mystery at all," Burke said bitterly.

"I won't keep you folks any longer," the sergeant said in an apologetic tone. "I know it's late. But I wanted to bring you the news. I'll be on my way now."

Roger was in an expansive, jubilant mood. "I'll see you out, Sergeant," he said.

As the two left the room, Elizabeth sighed and said, "Well, at least we can all sleep in our beds without worrying now." To Amos she added, "I'll go and prepare your room for you. I'll be back shortly." She left and Carolyn went with her.

Now only Victoria, Burke and old Amos Martin were left in the living room. Victoria had been gradually building up resentment all during Roger's baiting of them.

Now she spoke to the two men in a rage, saying, "How stupid can they be! Are you going to let them get away with it when we know better?"

"I think perhaps it might be best," Burke said quietly.

"But Mooney and that girl weren't to blame for what happened in Collinsport!" Victoria said angrily.

"It fits. They were in trouble with the police before they got here. Just suppose they escaped from the burning house through the rear door and stole a car."

"But it was Derek and Esther Collins who did all those awful things!" she insisted.

"We haven't an ounce of proof," Burke told her quietly.

Old Amos Martin had raised himself very straight in his chair and now he was staring at the portrait of Derek on the wall in front of him. In his rasping voice, he said, "When he and his woman died in the fire tonight that ended it. Better let it be the end of it." He smiled sardonically. "No good having people call you mad, same as they do me."

Victoria shook her head. "But to have to deny what we know!"

"What we know," Burke said. "The three of us. Let it remain that way. It's sure to be easier all around."

She studied the faces of the two men who had shared the days and nights of tension and horror with her. Burke's handsome face was grave and pleading. Old Amos Martin's eagle-like countenance showed a sad, resigned smile. And she saw they were right. An easy explanation had been provided. They would gain nothing by insisting on the acceptance of a more difficult one.

She said, "If you both think best."

"We do," Burke said. "And now it's time for me to go." He said goodnight to the old man and promised to return the next day to discuss his future plans. Then he and Victoria started out.

They met Roger on his way into the living room again after seeing the sergeant to his car. The blond man gave them a mocking smile that was strangely reminiscent of the one on the face of his ancestor Derek in the portrait.

"Well, I guess that settles everything," he said.

"I'm sure it does," Burke said quietly. Roger looked slightly astonished at receiving no argument and went into the living room.

Victoria and Burke said nothing until they were outside. The night had gotten cooler. In the distance, far down the beach, the burning embers and smoke from the fire could still be seen. She stared at the fading blaze for a long moment.

Then she turned and said solemnly, "I'll never forget tonight."

"Nor will I," he said gently.

"I suppose we shouldn't even talk about it anymore," she said.

"That would make it easier, I think."

She looked up at him with gentle eyes and said, "Thank you, Burke, for everything. I guess this is the end of a chapter."

He smiled. "But by no means the end of the story." And he took her in his arms for a lasting kiss.

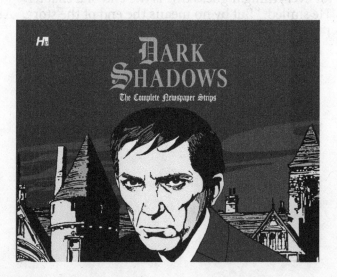